Possession

An Emily Chambers Spirit Medium Novel
#2

C.J. ARCHER

19/12

FOR

Joe, Samantha & Declan.

And for readers. Everywhere.

.

CHAPTER 1

London, Spring 1880

Someone watched us. I don't know how I knew. I just did. It wasn't a ghost because I couldn't *sense* spirits, only see them. No, someone real and very much alive was following us home.

It wasn't the first time.

"Do you feel that?" I asked my sister, Celia, as I glanced over my shoulder. An elderly couple strolled arm in arm on the other side of the road, a middle-aged woman struggled with a heavy basket up to the front door of a house, and a man crouched at the feet of a girl to tie up her boot lace, their heads bent against the breeze. A black hansom rattled past and the horse lifted its tail and deposited its business on the street, adding to the smells of soot and dung already clogging the air. All seemed quiet. Nothing was out of place for a spring afternoon in residential Chelsea.

"Feel what?" Celia asked, her gaze set firmly on the way ahead.

"Like we're being spied upon."

She laughed. "Who would spy on us?" But her laughter died as soon as the words were out. She stopped and looked at me. "He's not back is he?"

There was no need to ask who "he" was. She was referring to Jacob Beaufort, eldest son of Lord and Lady Preston, a ghost, and the man I couldn't stop thinking about. I'd not seen him since we'd returned a shape-shifting demon to the Otherworld a week before. The Administrators in the Waiting Area—the place where spirits reside for as long as they need to before crossing over to the Otherworld—had assigned him to me when Celia accidentally released the demon during one of our séances. After the demon's return, Jacob had simply vanished. No matter how many times I tried to summon him, he did not reappear.

Perhaps he'd crossed over, but I doubted it. He was a rare ghost. Unlike others, he didn't know why he couldn't cross. Something was keeping him in the Waiting Area, something more personal than the temporary demon hunting assignment. It was likely related to his mysterious murder.

"No, it's not Jacob." My voice cracked despite my effort to control it.

Her gaze narrowed. She sighed then circled her arm around my shoulders, squeezing gently. "It gets easier in time."

How would you know? Celia was thirty-three and unwed. She'd had admirers but never accepted their offers of marriage, despite our mother's encouragements when she was alive. Celia claimed she didn't love any of those men enough to marry one. It was a decision that resulted in her now being firmly on the shelf. I used to think she was foolish risking spinsterhood by waiting for love. To me, falling in love was like being struck by lightning. You knew it happened to some people, just nobody you'd met.

Or that's how I used to think before I met Jacob. Almost from the moment I saw him, I knew I loved him. What we shared had been magical, wonderful. All the clichés from every poem I'd ever read didn't come close to describing the feeling I had when near him. He set my nerves on fire, made my body ache and filled my heart with so many emotions I thought I'd burst.

When he was gone, it was like someone had thrust their fist into my chest and wrenched out my heart. I couldn't imagine the ache ever lessening, let alone disappearing completely.

As we turned onto Druids Way, the feeling of being watched vanished. Nevertheless, I remained alert the rest of the walk home.

Our house was nestled between identical terrace houses lining the street. Most were in need of painting or fixing here and there to tidy them up. For some reason, Druids Way was the forgotten child of Chelsea. The fashionable no longer lived there and our neighbors were elderly, having moved in before Queen Victoria came to the throne. The wind tugged at our skirts and ribbons and Celia let go of me to hold onto her bonnet. Her other hand clutched the carpet bag that carried our props for the séance we'd just conducted.

We reached our front door without hats or ribbons blowing away and were met by Lucy. The maid's eyes danced with excitement and her milky complexion flushed a rosy pink.

"Miss Chambers, you've got visitors!" she said, taking our bonnets. "Very fine they are too. Her ladyship's dress is—"

"Her ladyship!" Celia and I said together.

Lucy nodded and hung our bonnets on the hallstand. "I put them in the drawing room and offered them tea. They insisted on waiting, see, and I couldn't very well say no since she's a lady and all."

"Who?" I asked.

"Didn't I say? Lady Preston and Miss Beaufort, her daughter."

Celia's gasp was barely audible over the loud thud of my heart. I pressed a hand to my chest and tried to breathe normally but failed miserably. Lady Preston was Jacob's mother. Last time I'd seen her she'd hit an assailant over the head with a candelabra, saving my life and—unbeknown to her—the soul of her son who was doing battle with the demon. Prior to that she'd not believed me when I said I could speak to Jacob's ghost. She'd refused to accept his death, and her husband had put down the events of that evening to trickery and good acting on my part.

So what was she doing in our house?

"She's so fair and pretty," Lucy gushed, clutching our coats to her bosom. "The daughter I mean, but her ladyship's still pretty for her age too, and *so* elegant."

"Never mind that," Celia said with a wave of her hand. "Tell me you used the Wedgewood tea service."

"I did, Miss Chambers."

"Good girl." Lucy beamed. "Come, Emily," Celia said to me. "Let's see what Lady Preston wants." As we started to leave, she caught my arm and held me back. "Do not, under any circumstances, mention that Jacob boy. Mothers don't like to hear about the...friendships their sons have with girls."

I nodded and refrained from telling her mothers probably didn't like hearing about their dead sons at all, particularly Lady Preston. Last time Jacob's name came up, I thought she'd scratch my eyes out for suggesting he wanted her to move on with her life.

We entered the drawing room and I knew immediately Lady Preston was perhaps, just perhaps, coming to terms with Jacob's death. She gave me a tentative smile without an ounce of hostility in it. Beside her on the sofa, Adelaide Beaufort grinned and I couldn't help returning it. It was so nice to see Jacob's sister again. She was a sweet girl of about my own age and had believed me when I said I spoke to Jacob's ghost. It would seem she'd talked her mother into believing it too.

I introduced them to Celia then sat on one of the chairs bracketing the hearth. Celia sat on the other. Lucy must have lit a fire in the grate when our guests arrived as there hadn't been one when we left. Our séance business was not yet successful enough for us to end our economizing and keep a fire burning while we were out in the springtime. Nor had we been able to afford new furniture, much to Celia's disappointment. I admit it was a little embarrassing having illustrious guests sitting on our faded sofa, the threadbare carpet at their feet. Thankfully we'd both worn our better day dresses to the séance.

"It's so lovely to see you again," Adelaide said. Her bright blue eyes, so like her brother's, danced merrily, making her look even prettier. She was fairer than Jacob with honey-colored hair that curled delicately at her temples and ears. Not at all like my black springy mane that never stayed in place and skin that never paled no matter how much lemon juice I applied. "I do hope you've been well."

We exchanged pleasantries and drank our tea, but it wasn't long before the conversation turned to their reason for visiting. It was exactly what I thought it would be.

"Miss Chambers," Lady Preston said, her voice so soft I had to strain to hear her, "I hoped...that is, I wondered...if..." Her voice faded and tears sprang to her eyes.

Adelaide took her mother's hands in her own. "We wondered if you could...summon Jacob's ghost for us," she finished.

I couldn't actually hear Celia groan, but I could sense it. It's not that she didn't like Jacob. It's just that I couldn't wed a dead man, and according to her, it was time I began to think about my future.

"Emily?" Adelaide peered at me through those wide eyes. "Is everything all right? He hasn't...what do you call it when a ghost moves on?"

"Crossed to the Otherworld," I said. "No, I don't think so. It's just that I'm not sure if he'll come when I summon him. I've tried, you see, and he...hasn't." I picked up the teapot and refilled my cup, but my hand shook and tea sloshed over the sides.

"Are you sure you want to speak to him, Lady Preston?" Celia asked, all sweetness and understanding. She was as good at the sympathy part as she was at the exuberant theatrics of the séance. Distressed family members often found comfort in her kind words and gentle voice. Lady Preston was no exception. She gave Celia a watery smile. "It won't be easy for you both," my sister went on. "Indeed, it might be quite traumatic even though you can't see him or speak to him."

"We'll be all right," Lady Preston said. "We *need* to speak to him. You do understand don't you, Miss Chambers?"

I understood that need very, very well.

"We'll pay you of course," Adelaide added.

"No, please, I don't want payment," I said. Celia gave a small, exasperated sigh, but I ignored her. "Jacob is a friend and I want to see him too." He might not want to see me, but hopefully he'd make an exception for his mother and sister. I cleared my throat and drew a deep breath. "Jacob Beaufort, come to us. I summon Jacob Beaufort to appear in this realm."

A moment passed. Two, three. Lady Preston lowered her head and pressed a dainty gloved hand to her nose. Adelaide nodded, wordlessly imploring me to try again.

I opened my mouth but didn't get a chance to speak. Jacob appeared near the door, his arms crossed over his chest. My breath hitched at the sight of him, so handsome with his dark hair, strong jaw, and lips I wanted to touch with my own. He wore black trousers and a shirt unbuttoned to his chest, revealing a patch of skin as smooth as polished oak. Like all ghosts, he wore the clothes he'd died in, and his knuckles bore the cuts and bruises incurred during his last violent moments alive.

I gripped the arms of my chair to stop myself from running to him and throwing myself into his arms. From the coolly bland expression on his face as he regarded me, I didn't think my exuberance would be welcome. We'd not parted on the happiest of terms.

"Emily?" Celia prompted. "Is he here?"

I nodded.

Lady Preston gave a wet gasp. "Jacob?" She glanced around the room, her damp eyes searching the afternoon shadows.

Adelaide shifted forward on the sofa. "Where?" she whispered.

I indicated the doorway, but Jacob had already moved, making his way slowly to his mother and sister. Where before his features were carefully schooled, they were now stripped of the mask. Sadness tugged at his mouth and clouded his eyes as he knelt by his mother. His hand hovered over hers, clasped in her lap, and I was surprised to see her gaze lower to look directly at him as if she could see him there. She couldn't possibly see him or feel his hand on hers, but somehow she just knew.

"Jacob?" She reached out and her fingers went straight through his cheek. "You're here." She spoke with quiet wonder, her eyes wide and unblinking.

Jacob tilted his head slightly as if leaning into her hand, but of course it only sank further into him. Aside from me, he'd not touched another living soul since his death nine months ago. He must have ached for it.

"Perhaps you should hold something," Celia said in the general direction of Jacob's ghost. "So we know where you are."

His chest inflated, but not for an intake of breath as he no longer required air in his lungs. I'd learned there were some things the ghostly body did naturally out of long habit rather than necessity.

"Of course," he said, rising. He leaned down and kissed the foreheads of his mother and sister, but neither made any sign that they knew it.

If only he would kiss me. I'd even settle for him looking at me, but he didn't do that either. Was he going to ignore me the entire visit? That might be difficult, as I was the only one who could communicate with him.

We'd parted awkwardly after we'd sent the shape-shifting demon back to the Otherworld. I hadn't wanted him to go, not until we'd solved the puzzle of his death, but he no longer wanted to be near me. He thought he would put me in danger because he wanted to be with me, always, and my death would secure that.

He stepped around the furniture to the mantelpiece and picked up the framed daguerreotype of Celia's father as he always did when he was in our drawing room. I say Celia's father and not "our" father because he wasn't mine. He'd died a year before I was born. My parentage was a mystery, as my mother hadn't remarried after her husband's death and there didn't seem to have been any lovers.

"Oh, Jacob." A wide grin split Adelaide's face. She shook her head and shrugged. "There's just so much to say...where do we start?"

Lady Preston smiled at the picture frame, blinking rapidly. I didn't think any questions would be forthcoming from her quite yet.

"Jacob?" I prompted. His gaze flicked to mine then back to his sister. He nodded, understanding he must carry the conversation until they regained their wits.

"Ask them if they are well," he said.

I did.

"Oh yes," Adelaide said. "Quite well." She touched Lady Preston's hand. "Mother was...out of sorts for quite some time but regains more vitality every day." There was no need to elaborate. We all knew Lady Preston's ill health had been caused by her son's sudden disappearance and her inability to accept his death.

"Father is well too," Adelaide went on, her enthusiasm spilling out of her as she grew more comfortable. Unlike me, she didn't sense Jacob's mood darken at the mention of his father. They'd not been close during Jacob's lifetime, and the son's dislike of his father had only increased after he witnessed the cruel way Lord Preston had treated me.

"Ask her if she's attended many balls," he said, leaning against the mantelpiece, looking very much like the man of the house. "How many gentlemen have offered for her hand already?"

I asked Adelaide if she'd attended any Society events and

she launched into a list of balls, dinners and even breakfasts she'd been invited to since Lady Preston announced the end of their self-imposed seclusion.

"Your sister is going to have a ball for her coming out," Lady Preston said. She twisted her fingers in her lap and delicately chewed on her bottom lip. "It's not that we've forgotten or have set it behind us..." Her voice trailed off and she pressed her hand to her nose again. "I will wear full mourning of course."

"I know," he said quietly. "Emily, assure her this is what I want. It's time Adelaide enjoyed herself."

"That makes Jacob very happy," I said to his mother and was rewarded with a small smile from her. "He wants Miss Beaufort to attend parties."

"Oh, I shall," Adelaide said. "But I'll miss him. It won't be the same without him there to introduce me to his friends and other people whose names he can't remember but pretends he does." She smiled sadly.

"She knows me too well," he said drily.

It was certainly no laughing matter as Jacob's inability to notice people outside his immediate social circle may have inadvertently led to his death. We'd connected his murder to a boy from his Oxford year, known only as Frederick. The boy had thought Jacob was avoiding him, when in truth Jacob hadn't really noticed him. This perceived slight had led Frederick to set upon Jacob, only to come off worse in the fight. Although he'd gotten up and run away, Jacob's murderer had later made it known that Jacob was "responsible" for his—or her—son's death. Jacob assumed the killer was speaking of Frederick and the boy must have died some time after the fight.

But it was all speculation. No one really knew why Jacob had died.

"We want to find your body," Lady Preston blurted out. We all looked at her. She looked at the daguerreotype in Jacob's hand. "And to do that we must ask your...your..."

Killer. "Yes!" I said, perhaps a little more enthusiastically than was polite considering the circumstances. "I agree, Lady Preston." I raised an eyebrow at Adelaide.

She nodded. "I told Mother and Father about that Frederick boy and how his parent might be involved. Father said...well, never mind his exact words, but he's not interested in following that line. He says his detectives are being paid well and will discover who the murderer is without your...our intervention."

Lady Preston winced. "However, I think you might be right about this Frederick, Miss Chambers."

"It was Jacob who made the connection. I'm just his voice," I said.

"Don't disregard your role, Em," he said. It was the first time he'd spoken directly to me since his appearance and it caught me off guard. I couldn't think of anything to say.

"Do you mean you will hire detectives of your own, Lady Preston?" Celia asked.

Lady Preston shook her head. "I came here to speak to Jacob, to urge him to think very hard about who precisely Frederick is, or was."

"He has tried," I said. "He can't recollect him. Perhaps if we made discreet enquiries, someone at Oxford may know of him."

"My thoughts exactly," Adelaide said.

"No." Celia spread her fingers on her lap, a sign she was trying very hard not to raise her voice. "Absolutely not. You are not to get involved, Emily. This is a matter for others, not young ladies."

"Agreed," Jacob said with all the coldness of mid-winter in his voice. I wrenched my gaze from his but shivered nevertheless. I didn't want to argue with him over the point, but I would if I had to.

"I'm not suggesting your sister be involved at all," Lady Preston assured Celia. "Just that she communicate with Jacob and learn as much from him as possible. I'll write to his old friends and see if they know of any Fredericks. If that fails, I'll write to the university itself and obtain a list of all

Fredericks in Jacob's year."

"A sound idea," Celia said, relaxing.

No, it wouldn't do. Not at all. Letters would not suffice, and I would not be shunned. The investigation was too important. "I'm not sure letters are quite personal enough for this task." I turned to Jacob. "Is there one friend in particular who might know about this Frederick fellow? Someone popular with a wide circle?"

He narrowed his eyes. "What are you getting at, Emily?"

"Just that a visit to one person might be more appropriate and discreet. In fact, I'd go even further and suggest that you be the one to visit him, not your mother or sister."

"Ah." He crossed his arms and his lips tilted in a sardonic smile. "I see now. If I agree then that means *you* have to attend too as my medium. A good try, but the answer's no. I'll not involve you."

"Because it's not my business?" I spat.

"Because I don't want you to get hurt."

A little late for that. My heart hurt like the devil ever since he'd suddenly appeared in my life then just as suddenly disappeared.

Celia coughed politely and I apologized for my one-sided conversation. "But I do think it's a good idea," I added. "And yes, it necessitates that I go too, but it's just a simple visit and will be one time only."

"I don't think it's wise," Celia said, but she was wavering. I could tell by the way she studied her teacup and didn't meet my gaze.

"I'll chaperone her," Lady Preston said quickly.

"I'll go too, of course," Adelaide added. "It'll be quite safe. As Emily said, it will be very discreet this way. No one will ever know we're making enquiries and I do think Jacob's guidance will be invaluable."

"Ha!" Jacob barked. "Bloody female logic. I don't suppose I have any say in this."

"Jacob agrees to the scheme," I told them.

Another harsh laugh from Jacob's direction. I ignored him. It seemed the best course of action while in public. Now if I could get him alone...

"Excellent." Lady Preston rose and smoothed her black basque jacket over her hips. "Come tomorrow, Miss Chambers. In the mean time, if you could tell her which of your friends will best serve our purposes, Jacob, that would be most helpful." It seemed our new endeavor had indeed brought Lady Preston back to life, and I found I liked her very much. I could believe this forthright woman was the mother of two charming, remarkable people better than the shadow I'd met over a week ago.

Our guests—the live ones—said their goodbyes. Celia and I walked them to the front door like old friends. Jacob remained behind in the drawing room, or perhaps he'd already vanished back to the Waiting Area. At least he would return to give me the name of someone to contact. It would give us a chance to finally talk. Alone.

I opened the front door and the familiar feeling of being watched returned. I tensed, looked left then right. At the corner of the street, peering back at us from behind the red-brown bricks of the largest house on Druids Way, was a little girl. It was too far to make out much except that she had black hair, a black coat, and couldn't have been more than about ten. It was the same girl whose bootlace was being retied by the man earlier.

"Excuse me," I said, moving down the stairs past Adelaide. "I must speak to that girl."

"Emily!" Celia scolded. "Our guests are just leaving."

I held my hand up for her to wait and began to run, but before I reached Mrs. Norstrop's house two doors down I saw the little girl's mouth move, uttering words I couldn't hear. An edge of something black—a coat?—flapped beside her, but the rest of it was out of sight around the corner.

Behind me, someone grunted.

"Adelaide!" Lady Preston cried out.

I spun round to see Celia supporting Adelaide and Lady

Preston flapping a hand at her daughter's white face. Jacob hovered anxiously nearby and I knew he wished he could help.

"She almost fainted," he said, pacing around her.

Adelaide shooed Celia and her mother away, but she swayed unsteadily. "Bloody hell," she muttered, pressing both hands to her temples. "My bloody head hurts."

"Adelaide!" Lady Preston gasped. "Language."

Celia coughed politely and looked away. Jacob stopped pacing and stared at his sister as if she were a creature from another world.

Adelaide put a hand over her mouth. "Oh! Oh, I can't believe I said that. I'm so sorry, Mother, really. I don't know what came over me." She closed her eyes and groaned loudly.

"I think we should go home," Lady Preston said. "It's been a draining day."

"Would Miss Beaufort like to return inside and rest?" Celia asked.

"No." Adelaide sliced her hand through the air. "Let's go."

I suddenly remembered the little girl. I looked up the street, but she was gone. Curses!

"Until tomorrow, Miss Chambers." Lady Preston took her daughter's arm. Adelaide's face screwed up and she regarded her mother with disdain. With a snort and deep laugh that made my spine tingle, she marched down Druids Way with long, purposeful strides. Lady Preston had to trot to keep up.

Jacob watched them go, a frown cutting across his forehead. "Strange," he muttered. "Very strange."

"Did you see her?" I asked. "That girl at the corner? Did either of you see her standing there? I think she's the one who's been watching me."

"Someone's been watching you?" Jacob asked, his full attention on me. "For how long?"

"Ever since..." *you left.* "For about a week."

"Why didn't you tell me?"

I thrust one hand on my hip and stalked across to him so that we were close enough to touch. Dear God, how I wanted to touch him, but he'd made it clear there would be no more intimacy between us. My frustration made me speak harsher than I meant to. "If you'd come when I summoned you, I might have."

He had the decency to look away. "Well, I'm here now," he said softly. "Tell me about the girl watching you."

"There's nothing to tell. Today is the first time I've seen her. She was just a little girl, only..."

"Only what?"

I shook my head. "Nothing. She was too far away to see clearly." And I might have imagined the dark, wild curls and the darkish skin, so like my own.

CHAPTER 2

"Celia," I hissed when we returned to the drawing room. "Can you leave us alone for a few minutes?"

"Certainly not! That would be entirely inappropriate." She sat in an armchair with a dramatic puff of skirts and settled herself back as if she were putting down roots. There would be no moving her.

"It doesn't matter," Jacob said from where he stood at the fireplace, his back to us. He clasped his hands behind him and stared into the glowing embers as if he could see answers there. Answers to what? What the future held for us?

But we had no future together. Not until...not until I died and joined him.

"I'm leaving as soon as we finish discussing this business," he added.

"But you can't!" I went to him and put my hand on his shoulder. He stiffened and shifted away. My touch might as well have burned him. I let my hand drop to my side. "You can't go," I said, quieter. "Not yet."

Celia began to hum out of tune.

Lucy entered and I snapped my mouth shut. Her interruption was probably for the best as I'd been about to say something to my sister I would regret later. The maid collected the tea things, made a few awed comments about our elegant lady guests and their fashionable clothes then left with the tray, none the wiser about Jacob's ghostly presence. Just as well. She looked a sturdy girl, but spirit matters made her nervous. She could not yet bring herself to be alone with me.

I couldn't really blame her. My talent for seeing the dead was certainly unnatural. I'd not heard of anyone else with the ability. There were many who claimed they could, particularly in London where mediums were becoming as popular as the bearded dog lady for entertainment, but I'd yet to hear of one who wasn't a charlatan.

"I've been thinking about an appropriate friend for you to call upon," Jacob said, "and I've decided Wallace Arbuthnot will do. Mother knows the family a little. If anyone knows who this Frederick fellow is, it will be him. Arbuthnot likes to put his nose into everyone's business, but he's a good man. He should be on holiday from university at this time of year. You'll find him at his parents' house in Kensington."

"Wallace Arbuthnot. Right." I wanted to say so much more, but all I said was, "Is that it?"

Celia cleared her throat and made a great show of picking up her sewing from the basket beside her chair. She started humming again. We couldn't fail to notice her, which was no doubt her intention.

Jacob inclined his head. "We've said everything there is to say, Em. Anything else at this point would be unfair to us both."

"No. We haven't said everything." I lowered my voice and moved closer. I wanted to run my fingers along his smooth cheek, rub away the tension in his shoulders, but I kept my hands to myself. Celia might not be able to see him, but she would know. "I've been thinking about why you want to stay away from me." He flinched as if I'd pinched him. "You said you were worried you'd...hurt me." What he'd actually said was kill me, but that was much too painful to say out loud. "I think you're wrong. In my experience, the deceased retain the characteristics of their life. A good man in life is a good man in death. You aren't capable of harming anyone, let alone someone you care about."

"Don't be so sure about that."

And then he was gone. Just like that, right in the middle of our conversation. It was most infuriating!

"Jacob! Jacob, come back!" I stamped my foot and clenched my fists. It was childish, but I didn't care.

"Has he gone?" Celia said idly, intent on her stitch.

"You know he is." I stormed out of the drawing room and up to my bedroom. I shut the door and flopped on the bed, too angry to cry. Angry that Jacob wasn't listening to his own heart, and angry that I cared so much.

***

Lady Preston's drawing room was much larger than our own, and much lighter thanks to the grand arched windows and the golden hues of the walls and furniture. She favored delicate, spindly chairs and tables, not the heavier modern pieces of most of our acquaintances. I liked the room very much, but after fifteen minutes waiting on my own, I'd run out of things to admire. The footman assured me her ladyship would be with me soon. "Soon" came and went. Countless minutes later Lady Preston finally hurried in, her fine features drawn tight.

"So sorry to keep you waiting, Miss Chambers," she said. "Adelaide is on her way down." Her gaze slid to the door through which she'd just entered and her frown deepened. "She might be some time yet." She turned a smile on me, but I wasn't fooled. I knew a polite, forced smile when I saw one. Celia had perfected it at our séances and I was learning quickly. "Did Jacob give you the name of a friend?" she asked.

I told her about Wallace Arbuthnot. "I know his mother," she said. "We'll go to the house directly." She glanced at the door again. "Once Adelaide appears."

Adelaide did not appear. We sat and waited, passing the time with idle chatter. I wanted to ask so many questions about Jacob's life, but I didn't know if his mother was ready to speak about him. I didn't want to plunge her back into melancholy.

Finally Adelaide entered the drawing room, the brown skirt of her plain satin dress bunched in one hand revealing rather more of her lower leg than was decent. Her other hand was pressed to her ribcage and her face was distorted in discomfort. Her gaze settled immediately upon me and she gave me an odd sort of grin, not friendly but somewhat...lascivious.

"Well, well. You again, eh?" she said in a gravelly voice. She sounded, and looked, like she hadn't slept well. Dark circles rimmed her eyes and her hair was already beginning to slip from beneath the hat. "Come on then, let's get this over with before these stays kill me."

She stalked out of the drawing room. Lady Preston and I glanced at each other. My shock was mirrored in her wide eyes. She muttered an apology then rushed after her daughter.

A large black coach pulled by matching grays waited for us outside. A footman held out his hand to assist Adelaide up the step. She ignored it and climbed in unaided. I took the offered hand and followed her. Adelaide patted the seat beside her and I sank into the cushioned leather. Then she did an even odder thing. She winked.

"Pretty little pet, ain't you?" Her tongue darted out and licked her bottom lip.

I shifted as far away as the seat would allow. Clearly she was out of sorts.

"Adelaide," Lady Preston snapped, taking the seat opposite us. The footman closed the door and the coach jerked forward. "Mind what you say in front of Mrs. Arbuthnot. If you so much as utter a single word out of turn, that busybody will ensure everyone knows of it by the end of the day."

Adelaide blinked rapidly and pressed her fingers to her forehead. "Yes, Mother. Sorry, Mother."

"Really, my dear, what has got into you? Ever since we left Miss Chambers' house, your behavior has been very odd."

Since my house?

Adelaide moaned. "I'm so sorry," she whispered. "I...I have a headache and feel quite...wrong somehow. I can't quite explain it. Dizziness and...and I find I can't recall everything."

"Perhaps you should remain at home," her mother said, softening. She leaned forward and peered into Adelaide's eyes. "You need to rest. I don't want you to fall ill."

"No!" Adelaide shouted. With a quick glance from me to her mother, she blushed and added, "I want to come. I'm just...not feeling myself yet. I slept poorly."

A sick feeling twisted my stomach. If Adelaide was not feeling like herself, then who was she feeling like? The fact this change had come over her after visiting me was twice as worrying. Thanks to my ability to see the dead, strange things seemed to be happening more and more of late. Perhaps the shape-shifting demon was back and had taken over her body, although I wasn't sure if that was possible while the victim was still alive.

I shuddered. Victims, demons...it was all so gruesome.

Fortunately she seemed to have returned to her normal self and she asked me about my recent séances. I chatted more to ward off awkward silences than anything else. Adelaide and her mother contributed little to the conversation and although they kept up polite façades, I suspected neither was really listening.

The coach came to a halt outside a row of tall, slender, red and cream brick terraces joined together in a straight row. I followed Lady Preston and Adelaide out of the coach. This time we all used the assistance of the footman. We were met at the door by a starched servant and directed to a drawing room with views over the street and a collection of

Oriental artifacts placed around the room.

A matronly woman swathed in glossy black and leaning heavily on a cane entered. She walked with an awkward gait on feet much too small for her size. She reminded me of a pig on trotters, but I pushed the unkind thought aside lest a giggle escape.

When she saw Lady Preston and Adelaide, her thin eyebrows nearly leapt off her soft, round face. "Lady Preston, this *is* an unexpected surprise. I doubted my ears when Jenkins announced you, but here you are. And your pretty daughter too." Her gray eyes skipped briefly in my direction, but her smile never faltered. What she thought of me was hidden beneath a politely bland expression. "Sit, sit." She pointed to the sofa with her walking stick then proceeded to lower herself into an armchair, slowly at first, then finally plunging into the sumptuous velvet.

Lady Preston introduced me and I was relieved to see not a hint of recognition on Mrs. Arbuthnot's face. It would seem she hadn't joined in the latest fashion of afternoon séances for ladies like many of her set. She was, however, clearly curious about my presence. I wasn't introduced as a friend, cousin, ward, or any such thing, which seemed to fuel her curiosity more. Her puffy-lidded gaze frequently wandered in my direction despite her carrying on a conversation with Lady Preston.

The chatter ended abruptly when Adelaide's irritated sigh drew everyone's attention to her. "We're not here to gossip," she said in that deep voice that grated across my nerves. "Is the boy here?"

Mrs. Arbuthnot made a gargling sound in her throat. "Pardon?"

"Adelaide." Lady Preston managed to scold her daughter without raising her voice above a whisper. "She's been out of sorts since yesterday," she said to Mrs. Arbuthnot.

Mrs. Arbuthnot laughed too loudly for it to be genuine. "She's quite eager to see my Wallace, is she?" She called for Jenkins. The butler entered and bowed. "Fetch Wallace if you will. Tell him Miss Adelaide Beaufort has come calling. That should get him out of bed." She turned her smiling face on Lady Preston. "He rises rather late since his return from Oxford, I'm afraid. The unfortunate consequences of late nights at his club."

With a huff, Adelaide stood and made her way across the room with long, purposeful strides. She lounged against the white marble mantelpiece and picked up a blue and white Oriental jar. She weighed it in her hand, lifted the lid, peeked inside, then replaced it. She moved onto a black statuette and repeated the exercise. We watched her, silent.

"Nice things you got here," she said, studying the oil painting above the fireplace. I was no art expert, but the hunting scene looked very well done, the detail intricate and colors vibrant. "Bet that's worth a quid or two."

Lady Preston gave a small gasp of horror. Mrs. Arbuthnot looked equally horrified but managed a self-conscious laugh. "What a charmingly direct way you have, Miss Beaufort."

Adelaide grunted and admired a large round plate decorated with Oriental dragons. My bad feeling returned with a stinging slap. She was certainly not acting like herself.

I wished Jacob were near. I suddenly had a flurry of questions to ask him. I considered summoning him but dismissed the idea. Alarming Mrs. Arbuthnot at this point would be unproductive. So I silently willed him instead. Of course nothing happened. A summoning needed to be spoken aloud.

Thankfully the tension in the drawing room dissolved when a young man burst into the room. It had to be Wallace Arbuthnot because he looked very much like his mother, except taller and with a shock of thinning blond hair standing to attention. He already showed signs that he would be grossly overweight in years to come. I feared for the buttons on his red silk waistcoat and the collar of his shirt, both straining to contain the man within.

"Lady Preston, Miss Beaufort, delightful!" He smiled and

bowed to all of us, including me, and I instantly decided I liked him. He had such a friendly, kind face, completely without guile.

"It's lovely to see you again, Mr. Arbuthnot." Lady Preston held out her gloved hand. He took it and kissed it gently. "May I present Miss Chambers," she said, indicating me.

He bowed graciously. "Delighted to meet you, Miss Chambers."

"And you know my daughter, of course."

"Of course. How are you, Miss Beaufort?"

Adelaide said nothing but eyed him up and down then circled him twice, her hands behind her back, her bottom lip protruding like a shelf.

Wallace coughed into his hand and glanced at his mother. She lifted one shoulder.

Lady Preston looked mortified. "Adelaide," she said oh-so-politely, "perhaps you should sit. You haven't been well, remember? *Remember?*"

Adelaide paused and pressed a hand to her head. "Yes, I remember," she muttered and sank onto the sofa beside her mother. She sat with a rigid back, her ankles demurely crossed, and stared down at her lap.

"Wallace, ring the bell. Tea, Lady Preston?" Mrs. Arbuthnot asked as if nothing were amiss.

"No, thank you, not today."

Mrs. Arbuthnot ordered Wallace back and he sat opposite Adelaide on a pretty but narrow chair that creaked under his weight.

A tall young man entered. He paused inside the door when he saw us and bowed. "My apologies, Aunt," he said. "I didn't know you had guests."

Mrs. Arbuthnot beckoned him with a crook of her finger. "My nephew, Mr. Theodore Hyde. He's staying with us for a while." She introduced us and Mr. Hyde bowed again, a warm smile on his lips and a sparkle in his clear gray eyes.

The family resemblance between the two cousins was

evident in the eye and hair color, but that's where it ended. Theodore was tall and lean while Wallace was shorter and round. Theodore's face looked like finely worked porcelain, Wallace's resembled a lump of clay. If the latter was jealous of the former's good looks, he didn't show it. Indeed, he greeted his cousin eagerly.

"Back from your walk already, Theo?" To us, Wallace said, "Theo likes to go for a brisk walk every morning. For fresh air, he says, but I tell him he won't get fresh air here in London." He laughed and his entire body shook. "He's from the country." As if that explained it.

Theodore laughed too and shrugged. "The air here is indeed an acquired taste. It might take a little more than my first week to get used to it. The exercise does me good, however, and I will not be put off by a bit of soot." He spoke with the crisp vowels of the upper classes, but a hint of a country drawl underpinned his words.

"Where are you from, Mr. Hyde?" Lady Preston asked.

"Shropshire, in a lovely part of—"

"My sister's husband has a small parcel of land in that county," Mrs. Arbuthnot said over him. "They wanted Theo to broaden his experience and discover new prospects here in London."

Wallace shifted uncomfortably in his chair, causing the legs to groan in protest. The only indication Theodore made that he was hurt by the note of condescension in his aunt's explanation was to lift his chin a little.

So he was proud. Proud but poor. I didn't need Mrs. Arbuthnot to tell me that. I'd already noticed his waistcoat was made of wool, not silk like his cousin's, and his shoes were worn down at the heel. I suppose it was Mrs. Arbuthnot's way to politely warn Lady Preston that her daughter shouldn't look at the handsome nephew when her son, the far better prospect, was in the same room. Not that Adelaide appeared to notice either man. She still stared at her lap.

"I've certainly managed to discover a great many things

here in London," Theodore said. The winning smile had returned to his face, lighting it up, inviting everyone to join in. It only made Mrs. Arbuthnot's frown deepen. "This city hums all day and night with activity. There's so much to see and do. It's a wonder you natives ever sleep!" His gaze swept between Lady Preston and Adelaide then finally settled on me.

I smiled and was rewarded with a slight reddening of his cheeks. He quickly looked away, but the blush deepened. My own face heated.

"This call is most unexpected, Lady Preston," Mrs. Arbuthnot said. "It is lovely to have you here, and your daughter. Isn't Miss Beaufort looking exceptionally well, Wallace?"

"Oh yes," Wallace said. "Very well indeed."

Theodore glanced at me and seemed surprised that I was looking at him. I was surprised myself. He grinned. I grinned back.

"Our call isn't entirely social," Lady Preston said. "We have a rather unusual question to ask you, Mr. Arbuthnot. It's regarding my son's...death." I wanted to applaud her for her courage. A little more than a week ago she wouldn't have admitted her son was dead and now she was even saying it out loud.

Nothing can put a dampener on a social call like a discussion about mortality. Mrs. Arbuthnot shifted and resettled her bulk. Wallace tugged at his cuffs. Theodore gave her his full sympathetic attention. "I see," Wallace said. He glanced at Adelaide, but she hadn't removed her gaze from her lap. He breathed out and one of his waistcoat buttons popped open. His stomach surged through the gap. "I am happy to assist you in any way I can," he said, earnestly. "Has there been any news from the investigators?"

Lady Preston paused before answering. "Some news has come to light, yes." She indicated me. "Miss Chambers has some questions she'd like to ask you regarding my son's Oxford days."

Mrs. Arbuthnot, Wallace, and Theodore all looked to me with renewed curiosity. "Miss Chambers is an investigator?" Wallace asked.

I quite liked the sound of that, so I nodded.

"Oh." Mrs. Arbuthnot's mouth turned down and her nose wrinkled up. To her class, an investigator was involved in a trade of the lowest kind, worse than a shopkeeper or clerk. Whether investigators were above or below spirit mediums on the social scale was anyone's guess.

"I would have thought you a little young to be an investigator, Miss Chambers," Wallace said.

"She's very good," Lady Preston said quickly.

"Oh no, I did not mean to imply she wasn't." Poor Wallace colored to the roots of his hair. "My sincere apologies, Miss Chambers. Now please, tell me how I can help. I'm eager to do what I can to uncover the circumstances surrounding poor old Jacob's demise. Good chap, he was." He turned wistful. "The best."

"Theodore," Mrs. Arbuthnot said, "be a dear boy and fetch Jenkins for tea."

He rose just as Jacob appeared behind the sofa where his mother and sister sat. Pleasure made me a little dizzy. I needed him, not only to help question Wallace, but to tell me if something had indeed taken over Adelaide's body. She seemed meek but for how long?

"Ask him about Frederick," he said. No "How do you do?" or "Is everything all right?" In fact, he didn't even look at me at all. He did, however, notice Theodore leaving the room. "Who's he?"

I couldn't answer him of course. "We've managed to connect Jacob's death to a boy who might have known him at Oxford," I said.

"Good grief!" Wallace sat forward and another waistcoat button slipped from its moorings. "Who?"

"A young man named Frederick, but we don't know his last name. We thought you might."

"Me?"

"We've heard you were very popular at Oxford."

He swelled and the final button fell victim, causing his stomach to part the waistcoat like a curtain. He didn't appear to notice. "I knew a great many people." He frowned. "Let's see, I can think of a few Fredericks, but only two were in our year."

"Have any of them died?"

"Well, yes, as a matter—"

Adelaide snorted, cutting off his answer. "Where'd the other one go?" She no longer gazed at her lap but fixed a rather derisive glare on Wallace complete with a curl of her top lip. "You'll have to do," she said in that grating voice I suspected wasn't her own. A chill rippled down my spine.

"Pardon?" Wallace said.

"Adelaide?" Lady Preston touched her daughter's hand, but Adelaide shook her off and stood.

Jacob and I exchanged glances. "What's going on?" he said.

"She's not well," I said.

"That's it, of course," Lady Preston agreed. She must have thought I was offering an excuse to our hosts.

"Of course," Mrs. Arbuthnot echoed unconvincingly.

"Unwell? In what way?" Jacob watched his sister stalk across the room. She paused in front of Wallace, gripped his shoulder and squeezed.

"Ow!" Wallace jerked away and rose. "Miss Beaufort, I—"

"Weak," she said, "but you'll do."

"Emily." The sharpness of Jacob's tone drew me to my feet. He strode toward Wallace and Adelaide amidst protests and pleas from Lady Preston to her daughter. "Emily, something's wrong," he said.

"Adelaide," I said with false cheerfulness, "we must go now."

She ignored me as a rush of air whipped at her drab brown skirt and teased her hair. With a small cry, she stumbled back. I steadied her and directed her to sit on the sofa again. Jacob knelt in front of her, utter anguish imprinted on every feature.

"Adelaide!" Lady Preston cried. "Dear Lord, not you too. Addie!"

"I'm all right, Mother," Adelaide said weakly, sitting up straighter. "I feel...better."

"Same here," said Wallace in a voice much coarser and deeper than his own. Oh God, no. No, no, no. Whatever had been in Adelaide must have moved to him.

"Were you feeling unwell too?" Mrs. Arbuthnot asked her son. "You should have said—"

"Shut up, you fat sow." That got everyone's attention. Mrs. Arbuthnot made a choking noise and pressed a hand to her mouth. Adelaide, Lady Preston, Jacob, and I simply stared at Wallace. He patted his round stomach, protruding from the waistcoat, and belched. "No more bloody stays," he said. "Weaker too. Easier."

"Who are you?" Jacob asked, approaching carefully. "Get out of my friend's body."

But Wallace made no indication that he'd heard him or could see him. "Good fortune and good health to you all, I'm off to have some fun." He grabbed a pretty blue and white vase from a table near the door and tipped the flowers and water onto the carpet. He tossed the vase from hand to hand then tucked it under his arm with a satisfied nod.

"Wallace Arbuthnot!" his mother boomed. Her voice was so loud and so unlike her softly solicitous one of earlier I worried something had taken over her body too, but then she apologized profusely to her guests and I suspected she was merely upset at her son's behavior. And with good reason. For a gentleman like Wallace to be so rude in the presence of ladies was sheer madness.

"I, uh..." Lady Preston, still grasping Adelaide's hand, stared at the door.

"I'd better follow him," Jacob said. "Something is very wrong." He vanished.

Theodore returned, glancing over his shoulder. "Is my

cousin all right?"

"Ummmm..." Mrs. Arbuthnot pressed a hand to her enormous bosom and stared after her son.

"Aunt?"

No one answered him, so I said, "Mr. Arbuthnot is going for a walk. For fresh air."

Theodore didn't look like he believed me.

"We'll return at a more convenient time." I lowered my voice. "Mrs. Arbuthnot, I'm sure you understand the need to keep the particulars of this visit quiet." She turned to me, shock still evident in her wide eyes and slack jaw. "We wouldn't want any unkind words spread about either Mr. Arbuthnot *or* Adelaide considering they are both...ill."

"Ill?" Theodore spoke cautiously, carefully. "My cousin wasn't ill when I left. What happened here?"

"Your aunt will explain," I said breezily.

Adelaide gave a little whimper and her mother helped her to her feet. They were both as white as fresh snow.

"Yes," Mrs. Arbuthnot said, rubbing the head of her cane. "Yes, of course." She shouted for her butler and he scurried in. By the uncertain look on his face, I expect he must have met Wallace in the hall. "See Lady Preston, Miss Beaufort, and Miss Chambers out."

"Miss Chambers?" Theodore took my elbow. He looked confused, concerned, and I wished I could tell him the truth. But I didn't want to alarm him or his aunt, and I wasn't entirely sure what the truth was anyway. "If there's anything I can do to help, anything at all, please let me know."

I thanked him. We left the house and climbed into the waiting coach. The footman closed the door and all three of us emitted deep, grateful sighs.

"What happened in there?" Adelaide asked. Her voice trembled as much as she did.

Lady Preston's arm circled her shoulders. "Nothing, dear. Absolutely nothing." Her gaze connected with mine and I nodded slightly. If she wanted to shield her daughter from the truth, then I was happy to go along with the scheme.

Except...what *had* happened?

Jacob winked into existence beside me. I went to touch his hand, resting on the seat between us, but he shifted away. So it was still like that, was it? All business. Very well. I could switch off my emotions too. I could.

I didn't want to tell the ladies he was here and alarm them—their nerves seemed frayed enough—so I simply lifted my brows at him and mouthed "What happened?" while they weren't looking.

"Possession." He watched his sister, sitting opposite. He might be a ghost, but his body still seethed with anger and frustration and God knew what other emotions. "A spirit took control of Adelaide's body then transferred itself to Wallace Arbuthnot. I don't know why or how, but all their movements were controlled by a spirit and not a very nice one if his manners were any indication. He's gone now. I couldn't find him."

It wasn't until the coach deposited Lady Preston and Adelaide back at their Belgravia house that I got to be alone with him. Lady Preston had ordered her driver to take me to Druids Way, despite my insistence that I could walk home.

"Are you all right, Em?" Jacob asked me as soon as the coach rolled forward.

"I would be if you'd only talk to me more, visit me." I turned to face him fully. "Jacob—"

"Don't!" He closed his eyes, sighed heavily. "Keep the conversation to the possession. Please."

I swallowed the barrel-sized lump in my throat. I wouldn't cry. I wouldn't. He was right to want to keep our conversation on a proper footing. Right but cruel. "Very well." I tried to remember all the questions I'd been bursting to ask before. "Oh yes. Why your sister? Why Wallace Arbuthnot?"

He opened his eyes. "I think the spirit preferred a man's guise to a woman's. As to why it chose him when it could have had any number of footmen or other men, I don't know. And as to why it chose my sister in the first place..."

He shrugged. "I can't answer that either."

"It has something to do with my house. There was a girl there." I pressed my fingers to my mouth. What I wanted to say was too fantastical, too absurd to contemplate. Yet I had to put it into words to understand it. "I think she summoned the spirit into Adelaide's body deliberately."

Jacob whipped around to face me. "What girl? Who was she?"

I shook my head. "I don't know, but I think she's the one who's been following me. There was a man with her too."

He dragged a hand through his hair, ruffling it. I got the feeling he was holding back from saying some very ungentlemanly words. "To what purpose?"

"I don't know," I said, weakly. Oh God, why didn't I take more notice of her? Why hadn't I confronted her and discovered her intent? "Nor do I know where to find her now. I'm so sorry, Jacob, I wish I was more useful."

He touched my hand and warmth instantly infused me, despite the coolness of his skin. "It's all right, Em. It's not your fault. We'll find out what's going on soon enough."

But not before Wallace Arbuthnot and the spirit inside him had done something terrible. Why else would a ghost of questionable morals possess someone in this realm if not to do harm?

CHAPTER 3

The coach turned into Druids Way and rocked to a rhythm set by the cobbles and the wind. It made for an uncomfortable ride. "I think I should pay George Culvert a visit," I said.

"Why?" Jacob asked.

"To learn more about possession."

"George is a demonologist, not a spiritologist."

"I'm quite certain that's not a word."

His gaze slid to mine. "I can tell you all you need to know."

George was an acquaintance of Jacob's—or had been when Jacob was alive—and a supernatural enthusiast specializing in demons. He had a vast library filled with ancient and somewhat strange books collected by his late father. Surely there'd be a tome or two on possession. It would be a good avenue to start our investigation, considering locating the girl and Wallace would be like finding two needles in two haystacks in a field full of haystacks.

I decided to call Jacob's bluff. "Very well. How does one get a spirit into a live person's body? And how does one then go about getting it out again?"

He crossed his arms. "I'll have to speak to the Administrators in the Waiting Area."

"Good. You do that while I visit George."

His lips thinned. "Why do you want to see him?"

"Why do you *not* want me to see him?"

The coach stopped and rocked as the footman hopped down. He opened the door for me, but I said, "There's been a change of plan. Please take me to Wilton Crescent, number fifty-two." The coachman would know it since it was not far from Lord and Lady Preston's house. The footman bowed and closed the door again.

"It seems you are determined on this." Jacob spoke to the door rather than me, his rigid jaw giving him an imperial aloofness that invited no friendship.

I reached out to touch him, but he flinched and I dropped my hand. "I am, but I fail to see why that is a problem."

The coach rolled off again, jerking us both. Jacob made a small sound in the back of his throat, half-groan, half-sigh. He tipped his head back, resting it against the cabin's wall. "You're right. Of course you are." He turned a sad but gentle smile on me. I should have smiled back, but there was something very, very wrong with the way he looked at me. "Go see George and ask for his help. He's a good man."

"Yes. Yes he is, but—"

"I have to go." He blinked off.

Now what could he have meant by that little exchange? First he acted jealous and then he praised George? It didn't make sense. Unless...

Oh. Oh no. He wouldn't dare try to pair me with George. Not after all we'd been through, all we'd said to each other.

Would he?

***

George carried a black and burgundy leather-bound book as long as my forearm and as thick as the drawer in the desk at which I sat. It made a solid *whump* as it hit the leather inlay on the desk's surface. There was no title on the plain cover so I opened it. The earthy smell of disuse and age wafted from the yellowing pages. It was pleasant, comforting, homely.

"*The Rapture of the Spirit and of the Mind: A Treatise on Dispossessed Spiritual Influences,*" I read.

"First published in the seventeenth century." George stood behind me and leaned over my shoulder. "Just like old times."

"The book?"

His face, so near mine that I could feel his breath on my cheek, colored. "No, I mean you and me. Here in my library. Doing this."

"Oh."

He pushed his spectacles up his nose and smiled. It was what Jacob had wanted—me to get close to George, to have him look at me as if I was a potential sweetheart.

It wasn't what I wanted. "Hardly 'old times,'" I said. "It was only last week."

He cleared his throat and straightened. "Yes. Only a week ago. You're right. Silly of me. Silly expression." He returned to the bookshelves and browsed the volumes, his hands behind his back, his head tilted to read the spines.

Oh dear. I'd hurt his feelings or offended him or perhaps both. Poor George. But he needed to know that I was not interested in him in that way. Encouraging him would be cruel—I had no intention of taking our relationship beyond friendship.

I carefully turned the brittle pages of the book. I was surprised to see it was done by hand considering it was written after the invention of the printing press. The lettering was beautiful. A loving and clever hand had painstakingly formed the curling script and drawn the accompanying illustrations. The artist's mind, however, was another matter. Image followed image of women with breasts exposed, grasping their hair or skirts as if they would tear them off, a look of either rapture or pain on their fair faces—it was difficult to tell which.

I glanced up at George, still standing at the shelves. Had he even read the book?

I turned the pages and the images became more obscene. He couldn't have read it. Naked couples performed lewd acts in positions a contortionist would have trouble achieving, and not all of the couples consisted of both a man *and* a woman.

George sat at the larger desk in the center of the library, away from me. Thank goodness. I couldn't possibly read the book without turning a bright shade of puce and drawing attention to myself.

Not all the illustrations were of vulgar acts, however. Some appeared to have the people committing murder or harm to others. It was horrid.

I concentrated on the text. The old form of the English language was difficult to understand, but after a while I became used to it. Most of the work was clearly inaccurate. For example, it suggested that possession by spirits came from eating part of the deceased's body!

A more useful fact it noted was that possession was never performed by good spirits as they were eager to crossover to the Otherworld and not disturb the living. It was only the evil, those without conscience when they were alive, who wanted to possess someone and make them perform terrible acts.

I read on until the bells of a nearby church struck half past twelve. The longcase clock from the entrance hall joined in. "Any luck?" George asked.

"Not really. You?"

He sighed and shut the book he'd been reading. "No. Most of these texts know less than us. It's all speculation. Perhaps Beaufort will come up with something."

I wasn't sure Jacob would disturb us if he did. Not if he wanted George and I to become closer...friends.

George rubbed his hand lovingly over the dark green leather cover of his book. "Emily." It sounded ominous.

"Yes?"

"I've been researching your kind."

"My what?"

"Your kind. Mediums. Conduits to the dead."

"Conduits to the dead?" The macabre phrase sent a chill through my bones.

"That's how one of these books put it." He waved a hand to encompass the shelves on the western wall of the library, densely packed with books from the ceiling, two levels above us, to the floor.

"And what did you discover about...my kind?"

"That you are a very rare breed indeed."

I am not a dog, I wanted to say but bit my tongue. George hadn't meant to offend. "Go on."

"There are a few known cases of legitimate mediums before the sixteenth century, but not many. The most famous one is actually referenced in the Bible, the First book of Samuel, chapter twenty-eight to be precise. Interestingly, that medium was a woman too. However, the fact we don't have more than a handful of cases does not mean more mediums have not existed, just that they weren't evident in our society."

"George, you're speaking in convoluted sentences. Please, tell me plainly." My heart rose into my throat where it lodged. I'd wanted answers to my parentage for so long, ever since I could remember, but now that some light was about to be shed, I wasn't sure I was ready to hear it.

He stood and climbed one of the ladders to the second top rung. He held onto one of the cast iron lamps attached to the shelf and reached up to remove a black book. "Here," he said, climbing down. "This is where I found the information."

He gave me the book and sat on one of the heavy armchairs nearby. I read the spine. "*Beyond The Grave: A Scientific and Historical Study of Death and the Spirit.*"

"The book is only fifty years old," George said, leaning forward and turning the pages quickly. "It gathers information from many sources over many years.

Unfortunately my father's collection doesn't have any of the original books so I cannot verify them. We have only this one to draw upon." He stabbed his finger at a page with the chapter heading "Conduits to the Dead."

I began to read. He settled back in his chair and crossed his legs. I could feel his gaze on me, but I soon forgot about him. The text was riveting. By the time I'd finished, my head was awhirl. I sat back and stared at the book. Where before my heart was in my throat, now it seemed to have stopped beating altogether.

George leaned forward and touched my arm. "Emily? Are you all right?"

I nodded and blinked slowly. "Do you think it's true? That there are women from an African tribe who can see the dead?"

"I have no reason to doubt it. But it's important to remember that these things may have been distorted over time and what we're reading here is just one author's opinion of sources we cannot read ourselves. But it seems...logical."

It did indeed. Being descended from one of the tribal women explained not only my ability, but my appearance too. It did not explain why there was a little girl running around who looked very much like me and was summoning ghosts into the bodies of live people.

"Miss Chambers, what a...surprise," came a throaty female voice from the doorway. Mrs. Culvert, George's mother, smiled a tight smile at us. I didn't believe it was sincere for a moment. "Greggs told me you were in here with George. Reading." Her icy gaze slid between us as if trying to determine if we'd been doing more than just reading.

I rose and curtsied. "Good afternoon, Mrs. Culvert."

Her smile flattened, her eyes hardened like two colorless diamonds. Clearly she wasn't sure whether to welcome me or ask me to leave. I was known to Lady Preston and her daughter, and therefore someone to be cultivated and exploited so that George could be thrown into Adelaide's circle. On the other hand, if George spent too much time with me, he might become enamored of a middle-class girl of dubious parentage instead, and that simply would not do for the ambitious Mrs. Culvert.

"Mother, would you mind ordering luncheon to be served for us in here?" George asked. "Emily and I have—"

"Oh, *Miss Chambers* is staying awhile longer?" There was no doubt she'd emphasized my name to draw attention to the informal way in which George had addressed me.

He bristled. "She is," he said, quite forcefully. It was almost defiance on his part. Good for George.

Her eyes narrowed to slits. Such a hostile expression would usually see small lines appear, but Mrs. Culvert's skin remained smooth, as if wrinkles didn't dare reside on her face. "But George dear," she said, frostily, "don't you think Miss Chambers would be more comfortable if she were chaperoned? I would offer to remain myself of course, but there is so much to do. I cannot linger here all afternoon."

"The door has always been open," George said, "and shall continue to be. Unless Miss Chambers feels uncomfortable...?" He looked to me, brows raised.

"I am perfectly comfortable." I was hardly a good enough catch that my reputation would be sullied by being with George in his library with the door open. The sort of man I was expected to marry did not move in the Culverts' circle and would never even hear about it. A woman of Adelaide's station lived by a different set of rules. Even the scent of a scandal was enough to ruin *her* chances of an advantageous marriage.

But I don't think Mrs. Culvert had my reputation in her thoughts at all. More like it was George's heart she was worried about. She shouldn't have worried. I did not want George to develop a fondness for me any more than she did.

"Perhaps I should go," I said.

"Not yet." George indicated the book. "We have much to discuss. I would not have you leave without...obtaining your opinion."

My opinion or my state of mind after all I had read in *Beyond the Grave?*

Jacob suddenly appeared near my chair and my heart almost burst out of my chest in fright. Fortunately I managed to suppress a squeal. "I agree with Culvert," he said. "Stay."

"Very well," I said to both Jacob and George. It didn't matter which. "Mrs. Culvert, thank you for your concern, but I am quite at ease here."

She sniffed and gave me that tight smile again, the one that thinned her lips and didn't reach her eyes. She moved to the door, her wide hem skimming the floor, giving the impression she was floating over the rug. The light filtering through the tall arched windows caught the dark green silk of her gown, adding depth and luster. The fabric would have been magnificent on a more fashionable dress, but Mrs. Culvert preferred the excessively puffed sleeves, low necklines, and voluminous skirts of years past.

"Oh Miss Chambers, I almost forgot." She paused in the doorway, the too-friendly smile back on her handsome face. "I believe Lady Preston is having a ball for her daughter. Is that not so?"

I glanced at Jacob. He stood unmoved nearby, his gaze not on Mrs. Culvert but on the book still open on the desk in front of me. "She mentioned it."

"Good, good." She cleared her throat daintily. Her smile didn't waver. "I'm sure Miss Beaufort will be guided by you, her friend, in this matter."

"Guided by me?"

"Yes, in the little things, as young ladies like to do. Things such as decorations, dresses...guests."

George groaned and sank into his chair.

Part of me wanted to laugh. It would seem Mrs. Culvert knew nothing about me at all. "I am not as close with Miss Beaufort as that."

It was as if I'd slapped her smile off. "Oh." She turned on her heel and stalked out the door.

None of us spoke until the *tap tap* of her heels on the tiles faded into the distance.

"Emily, I am terribly sorry," George said. "I do apologize. Mother can be rather caustic. She feels her lack of contact with Society keenly, you see."

"It's all right, George, I understand."

"If only she didn't care so much about forming the right connections for me. I don't."

According to George, Mrs. Culvert had the misfortune of marrying George's father, a man much like his son—devoted to his studies in the supernatural. The socially inappropriate pastime had seen Mr. Culvert's influence slip away and Mrs. Culvert ostracized by all who mattered to her. No wonder she was putting her hopes in someone with only a tenuous connection to Lady Preston. But to think I would be invited to Adelaide's ball was laughable.

"What's this about?" Jacob asked, indicating the book. If he'd been listening to the conversation with Mrs. Culvert, he made no comment.

"Spirits and the people who can see them," I said.

"Pardon?" George asked.

"Jacob is here," I told him.

George stood, puffed out his chest and squared his shoulders. "Good afternoon, Beaufort," he said, his voice a shade deeper than usual. I rolled my eyes. He was trying to impress Jacob, something that seemed to have carried over from Jacob's lifetime. When he was a student at Eton and then Oxford, many of his classmates had tried to gain his attention one way or another, so Adelaide claimed. Unfortunately, he'd rarely noticed them.

Jacob glanced at George. "Tell him I greeted him," he said. He picked up a quill pen from the brass inkstand so that George could locate him. "I want him to know I've acknowledged him."

I did as asked and gave Jacob a smile even though he wasn't looking at me. At least he was making an effort to rectify the shortcomings he'd possessed in life.

George puffed out his chest even further and pushed his glasses up his nose. "Have you learned something about possession, Beaufort?"

"A little," Jacob said. "The Administrators say only a medium can send a spirit into a live body."

I gasped. "*Only* a medium? You mean..."

"Someone like you, yes."

"But...but there *are* no others." Even as I said it, I knew it was wrong. If one such as me could be born then so could another. Aside from the little girl, how many others were there in the world?

"Emily?" George prompted.

I explained everything Jacob had said as well as our suspicions about the girl. George pursed his lips, grim. "This is terrible. Terrible."

I could not agree with him. The possibility of there being someone else out there like me made me giddy. I wanted to meet her. Talk to her. "She must surely be too young to know what she's doing." But I wasn't completely convinced. A ten year-old child was perfectly capable of mischief, and even malice, if she had the power and the will. Or there was the possibility someone was directing her.

"Do you know how to send a spirit into a person's body, Emily?" George asked.

I shook my head.

"It involves the medium uttering specific words," Jacob said.

I repeated this for George's sake. "But how did the medium transfer the spirit from Adelaide's body to Wallace Arbuthnot's? We were on the first floor of his house. No one could peer in through the windows."

"That was entirely the spirit's doing, not the medium's. The ghost apparently preferred Arbuthnot's body to Adelaide's. Thank God. But he wasn't able to transfer himself until they were touching. When that occurred, he simply jumped across. It's likely the medium doesn't know the spirit has moved on."

I finished repeating it all to George, then said, "How can the ghost be sent back?"

"If he won't go of his own accord, he can be forced. A medium must do it, but she needs to be within a certain proximity, just as she had to be nearby to force the spirit into my sister's body."

I swallowed. "Can a different medium do it to the one who summoned the spirit in the first place?"

He hesitated and failed to meet my gaze. That was nothing new. He'd not been looking me directly in the eyes ever since he arrived, but the small hesitation was telling.

"I can, can't I?" I said.

"You won't."

"Why not?"

"This isn't your business."

"It is. And you cannot order me about." I crossed my arms.

He crossed his. He met my gaze. His eyes were midnight blue and as endless as a starless night sky. "I can talk to the other medium as easily as I can talk to you. If I can convince her to reverse the damage she's done—"

"You have to find her first."

"I will."

I sighed. "Jacob, she is a little girl. You might frighten her. Besides, someone else may be directing her."

"That is precisely why I don't want you involved, Em." He spoke quietly and it was impossible to be angry with him. He cared for me, cared for my safety. Did that mean he no longer wanted me to die to be with him as he used to?

"I will find her on my own," he said. He waved his hand over the page in front of me. "Is this true?"

I looked down at the book, specifically at the illustration of a dark-skinned woman with wild black hair and large, knowing eyes. She wore what appeared to be a sack covering her body, but her feet were bare. The faint outline of a man dressed in the wide lace collar and broad brimmed hat of the seventeenth-century Englishman was sketched beside her.

They appeared to be having a conversation. A medium and the ghost she'd summoned.

"I don't see why not," I said. I tried to gauge Jacob's reaction, but his face was schooled and not a hint of his thoughts could be determined.

What did he think of me now that he knew I was descended from a tribe of mystics that originated in the deepest jungles of Africa? What did I think of it myself?

CHAPTER 4

After a brief luncheon and more research, I left George's house with Jacob at my side. I had a séance to conduct with Celia at three. Following that would be an intense interrogation of my sister. I had a thousand questions to ask her. She might not answer any, but I had to try.

"I'll search for Arbuthnot overnight," Jacob said. I suspected he was shortening his strides so I could keep up. He kept his gaze firmly on the footpath ahead, only disappearing once when a Royal Mail box was in his way. He simply reappeared on the other side of it. Passersby were a different matter. He could walk straight through them.

It was busy on Sloane Street. Carts and carriages of all sizes rumbled past, and fast drivers shouted at the slow ones to move aside or hurry along. Shoppers laden with parcels wandered in and out of shops and errand boys darted nimbly between the pedestrians and traffic. The cool air was thick with the scent of horse and soot. No sunshine broke through the gray miasma and if I didn't know it was spring, I couldn't have guessed at the season.

"The spirit didn't seem to see you at the Arbuthnots' house," I said quietly to avoid being noticed by strangers. "Why not, when you could see him?"

"His sight was limited to what the body he possessed could see. If he possessed you, he could see ghosts, but by occupying Adelaide and Arbuthnot, he could not. All the spirit's actions are now governed by what Wallace Arbuthnot can and cannot do."

"I suspect Wallace can't run up a flight of stairs."

"Or beat someone."

"Except in a pie eating contest."

He threw his head back and laughed. The sound was so good I joined in. "You're a wicked girl, Emily Chambers. Wallace Arbuthnot is a good man."

"Yes. He's very...solid."

We laughed until tears ran down my cheeks and a man behind me said, "Young lady, are you all right?"

My laughter died. My face burned and I couldn't meet his gaze. "Yes. Thank you. I was just...er..."

"Very strange," the man muttered, moving past me. "Talking to yourself like that. Very odd indeed."

"Never mind him." Jacob took my arm and escorted me across the road to where a young crossing sweeper pushed the horse muck aside with his broom. I thanked him and fished out a penny from my reticule to pay him.

Jacob let go of my arm. "All right?" he asked, without looking directly at me.

"Yes. Thank you," I whispered lest I be overheard again.

"Don't let them worry you. *You* know you're not mad."

"I might not be mad, but I am different."

His gaze met mine. "Yes," he murmured. "You are."

A fist slammed into my stomach, or so it felt. He didn't have to agree with me. Didn't he know how much I hated being different? He should if he knew me at all.

I trotted after him, his long strides making it difficult to catch up. When I was alongside him, he didn't look at me but straight ahead. We turned off the main thoroughfare and down a smaller residential street. It was quieter and I could speak to him freely without worry of being overheard. "Why are you avoiding me?" I asked.

"I'm not. I'm here. You're here. That's not avoidance."

"You won't look at me."

He looked at me. Briefly.

"Look at me properly."

"I need to see where I'm going."

I sighed. "Does this have something to do with what we just learned about me from George's book?"

He frowned. "No. Why would it?"

I shrugged. Perhaps his behavior had nothing to do with my ancestry. After all, he'd been acting distant ever since his return the day before. It was likely he was simply avoiding me because he wanted to end any feelings between us, so we could both move on.

I preferred that explanation to the alternative—that his infatuation was drawing to an end. *That* possibility was too horrible to think about.

"Emily, did you see anyone with the little girl when my sister became possessed?"

The change of topic threw me and I took a moment to gather my thoughts. "No, but I saw her earlier with a man. He was tying her shoelace and I didn't see his face. I assume they are the ones who've been following me lately."

"But why follow *you*? And why possess Adelaide?" Jacob huffed in frustration. "I suppose we'll learn soon enough when we locate Arbuthnot."

"How will you find him?"

He shrugged. "I'll try some pubs, but London is huge and without knowing who the spirit is, it's impossible to know where he might choose to go."

I drew in a deep breath and let it out slowly. Our task ahead was daunting, but I had something else on my mind. "Wallace Arbuthnot almost told us about Frederick before he became possessed. He said he was indeed dead, which is a start, but now we'll have to find someone else to help us. Your mother could write a letter to Oxford, but I don't think she wants to do that just yet."

"No," he said quietly. He dug his hands in his trouser

pockets. "Let's find Arbuthnot first and worry about Frederick later."

I didn't answer him. Part of me wanted Jacob to crossover, and I felt that solving the mystery of his murder would be the key to his moving on. But a very large part wanted him to stay here, with me. Perhaps it was selfish but it was the truth.

He paused at the intersection with Druids Way, almost at the same spot where the girl had summoned the spirit. "Emily?" I glanced up at him. He was looking down at me, his blue eyes bright but soft, warm. When he looked at me like that I felt like I was the most beautiful girl in the world. I could achieve anything, endure anything. "Emily, are you all right? That book...what you learned...it's a lot to consider."

I nodded and tried to smile. "I'm fine. It feels so far removed from me, like it's not about me at all." It was difficult to explain and in the end I simply shrugged. "The book answered some questions I had but threw up many more."

"I understand."

"Do you think a single tribal family had the ability to see the dead?"

He leaned against the iron fence of the corner house. A strong breeze ruffled his hair and flattened my skirt against my legs. The air smelled fresher in Druids Way thanks to the constant wind flushing out the soot. "It's plausible," he said.

The chapter had stated that only the females of the family could be mediums, but they did not pass the ability onto their children. It was the males who were responsible for perpetuating the talent down the family lineage. Their daughters inherited it and became mediums themselves, but their *sons* passed it along to *their* daughters and so on.

The tribe's unusual power became known to Europeans once exploration expanded in the fifteenth and sixteenth centuries, but even then it remained little more than a myth. During the later centuries, it seemed the tribe was almost wiped out from disease and slavery, although it was rumored many escaped due to their women's ability to cleverly summon ghosts to scare the slave traders away. For a while the tribe was thought to be lost, the family having died out.

But I knew differently. I was one of them. Very, very distantly if the lightness of my skin was an indication, but still one of them.

"That girl..." I said. "She might be...my sister."

"It's likely."

The ground shifted and I clutched the fence rail next to Jacob for balance. He touched my hand with his cool fingers. The simple gesture was more comforting than anything he could have said.

"We must find her," I said.

He squeezed my hand. "We will. Don't worry."

***

I did not question Celia until after supper. I tried plying her with an extra glass of wine but, frugal as ever, she refused. On to plan B, the direct approach. With the addition of compliments.

"Your performance today was wonderful," I said. We sat in the small parlor that we used when it was just the two of us. The fire burned low, its warmth enough to reach even the furthest corners of the room. Lucy had not yet joined us after finishing her chores, but she soon might and I did not want to have this conversation with her present. She was flighty enough as it was.

"Thank you, Em," Celia said, taking up her embroidery. She leaned closer to the lamp burning on the table beside where she sat in a well-worn armchair. I sat in the matching chair on the other side of the table, an open book on my lap. "It was a pleasant séance today, if a little sad. Mrs. Krump seemed to be much loved by her family."

"Indeed. And you made them all feel joyful about their elderly mother moving on. It was most ably and compassionately done. I have so much to learn from you."

She lowered her work and narrowed her eyes at me. "Would you like to ask me what is on your mind now, or do you have more compliments to pay me? Because I'm quite open to them, you know."

I gave her a withering glare and she smiled ruefully. "Very well, let me get to the point. I learned some things today at George Culvert's library."

She picked up her embroidery. "Oh?"

"I learned that I am descended from an African tribe."

She dropped her cloth, needle and all, and stared open-mouthed at me. She said nothing, but as I told her all that I'd read in *Beyond The Grave*, her face became paler until it was so white and pinched I thought she might faint. I knelt before her and took her hand. It was cold.

"Celia? Are you all right?"

"I...I...what you say...is it true?"

"I hoped you could tell me."

"I can't," she whispered. "I can't tell you anything."

I sighed. "I think you can. You know who my father was."

"*Our* father was a good man. He loved Mama—"

"Stop it!" I pushed her hand away and stood. "Stop it, Celia. Your father and mine are not the same person. I am seventeen and I am no fool, so stop treating me like a child!"

She blinked up at me. Her eyes were dry but dazed and distant. "You have grown up, haven't you?" She sounded surprised. "It's happened so slowly. I hadn't noticed until now."

"Then it's high time you told me all you know about my father. I deserve honesty."

"I suppose you do." She indicated I should sit back down then took up her embroidery again. Her hands shook. "He was indeed darker than most, a shade or two more than you, but I did not know of his African origins."

"Did Mama?"

She lifted one shoulder. "She may have."

"Go on."

Again the shoulder-shrug. "There's not much more to tell. Shortly after my Papa died, Louis, that was his name, came to work at his father's High Street grocery shop."

"Which one?"

"Mr. Graves now runs it."

I knew the shop and nodded at her to go on.

"There was so little money after Papa died that we had to let our maid go and do all the shopping on our own. Louis saw us struggling with our packages and offered to carry them home for us one day. Mama had been working so hard and I immediately accepted his offer even though she refused. He took it upon himself to listen to me and not her and carried our things. He refused our attempts to pay him.

"He was there the following week too and did the same, then the week after and the week after. We began to expect him to be present whenever we shopped and looked forward to his smiling face and friendly manner. He put us at ease with his chatter and charm and..." Her voice trailed off but her fingers sped up, pulling the thread so hard I thought it would break. "He was quite handsome too."

"So you became friends. Is that why Mama fell in love with him?"

She did not look up at me but kept stabbing the needle into the cloth with such fervor I began to worry she might stick her finger instead and bleed all over her lovely work. "I suppose so."

So my father was kind and generous. That at least was good news. Although it did seem strange that my mother would fall in love with another man, no matter how charming, mere months after losing her beloved husband. Perhaps she'd been lonely. "So who was Louis? What was his full name and where did his family come from?"

She drew in a deep breath and it seemed to steady her hand. "I know little of his family. I don't even know his last name. As I said, his father ran a grocery at the time. I hadn't seen Louis there before although I'd shopped there often with the maid. Louis simply appeared one day at a time when we needed him most. He was a bright spot in our otherwise saddened lives."

I sat back and regarded my sister. She seemed to think her tale finished, but I had more questions. "So what happened to Louis? Where did he go and why did he leave after Mama became pregnant with his child?"

Even with her head bent I could tell she winced. I knew how babies were made, but Celia had never liked that I knew, preferring to think of me as an innocent on that matter. "He left before the pregnancy became known."

"So why didn't Mama contact him? Did he not leave an address so she could write to him and tell him?"

"He went to the colony of New South Wales."

I gasped. "But that's on the other side of the world!"

"It is. But there was no life for Louis here. London doesn't like people who are...different."

I could vouch for that. "Why New South Wales?"

"There were opportunities there. Our government had a scheme whereby they paid the traveling costs of able-bodied people who wanted to move to the colonies. He applied and was accepted. He promised to send for us when he was settled, but we never heard from him again."

He could even be dead. An unexpected lump lodged in my throat and I couldn't swallow past it.

"We visited his father at the shop some time after you were born," Celia went on. She was rigid, her back as straight as a plank of wood, her eyes focused on her embroidery that she continued to work with alarming intensity. "We wanted to know if he'd heard from Louis. The old man said he'd received a letter in which Louis stated he no longer wished to have anything to do with his past life in London. He had made a new beginning in New South Wales and wanted nothing to...to ruin it." She held her embroidery at arm's length and studied it, her eyes bright in the lamplight. "There. Very pretty, don't you think?"

"Louis...my father...he never wrote to Mama? He never came back?"

She packed her needle and thread away in the basket. "Why would he? It sounds like he was quite content with

New South Wales. He didn't need the things he'd left behind."

Tears stung the backs of my eyes. My poor mother. "You did tell the old man about me, didn't you? I was his granddaughter after all."

"No. He...unnerved us. Mama and I never liked him. He had a strange way of looking at us, like he never trusted us. Perhaps he was so used to the prejudice that he could not identify kindness and friendship when it was genuine." She looked up as Lucy entered with a tray of tea things. "Ah," Celia said, cheerful, "perfect timing. A good cup of tea is just what I need."

I watched as Lucy poured the tea for each of us, including herself. My sister sipped then began a conversation with Lucy about the following day's meals. I hardly heard them. I was disappointed at first to have our conversation cut off prematurely, but I quickly changed my mind.

I did not want to tell Celia that Louis may have returned to London approximately ten years ago and fathered another child. She didn't need to know that he hadn't cared enough for Mama to see her again.

Perhaps it would have been different if he'd known about me. Then again, perhaps not.

I wanted to curl into a ball and brace myself against the tide of sadness washing through me. I got up and embraced Celia instead. I would always have her, and one family member was enough. After all, it was better than having none.

***

Jacob waited until after breakfast to tell me about his search for Wallace Arbuthnot. I was alone in the small parlor, Celia having already left to speak to Lucy in the kitchen. She and I had barely spoken over our coddled eggs and the weight of all she'd told me hung heavily in the air.

I wondered if Jacob timed his appearance with her departure. It wasn't that Celia disliked him. She just didn't like the affection I'd developed for him. As was often the case lately, her overprotectiveness had turned overbearing. I was glad to be alone with Jacob, even if we only discussed matters supernatural and not personal.

"I found Arbuthnot." He stood in the doorway, one broad shoulder resting against the frame. He looked relaxed and comfortable, until I noticed the tap of one finger on his thigh. It was a new habit he seemed to have formed.

"Thank goodness. Where?"

"Everywhere."

I slid my plate of coddled eggs away, no longer hungry. "What do you mean?"

"I mean the spirit inside Arbuthnot has taken him into gaming hells of the most disreputable kind, ratpits, pubs...think of the worst places in the meanest parts of the city and there I found him."

I stifled a gasp. "Poor Mr. Arbuthnot. If he knew what was happening to him, he would be utterly ashamed. He doesn't know, does he? Can he?"

Jacob shrugged. "My sister seemed to be partly aware when she was possessed, although dazed."

I nodded. "She was sometimes herself, but when the spirit had her fully in his grip, she seemed completely...gone. As if he'd overruled her mind somehow." I could think of no other way to explain it. It was as if Adelaide's will did not exist during the possession except for those brief moments when her mother's voice brought her back.

"Wallace is not as strong as Adelaide." That busy finger tapped his temple but then returned once more to drumming against his thigh. "It's possible he doesn't know what the spirit is doing."

"It's best that way."

"True."

I waited, but he did not continue. "So what are we to do now?" I asked.

He didn't immediately answer. I thought he would correct my usage of "we" to exclude me, but he didn't. Intriguing.

"You must tell me, Jacob. I need to know what to wear."

He burst out laughing and pushed off from the doorway. "Only a female would think of clothing at a time like this."

I gave him a withering look. "Would it be a good idea to enter a ratpit dressed in my good day dress?"

"You are not entering any ratpits."

"But you have found him, otherwise you wouldn't be here. You need my help, Jacob Beaufort. Admit it."

He clamped his jaw so hard I could hear his back teeth grinding. "I have found him, yes, but George will lure him to a place where you are waiting. A safe, respectable place."

It made perfect sense. Almost. "So I assume you will tell me where to find Mr. Arbuthnot and I will inform George. George will then go to that place and convince the spirit to follow him."

"Ye-es." From the cautious way he said it, I could tell he knew I had doubts and was waiting to hear them.

"I can see two flaws in the plan. No, three. Firstly, what if Arbuthnot has gone? Even if you manage to find him again, how will you communicate that to George without me there? It would involve George returning to wherever I am tucked away, waiting for you, you telling me—"

"All right." He held up his hands. "Point taken. Let's worry about him moving when and if he does. The other two concerns?"

I *humphed* at his dismissal. "Secondly, how will meek-mannered, gentlemanly George coerce a thug like that spirit into going with him?"

"Bribery."

"Which brings me to my third point."

"I had a feeling you would think of everything." Most men would have made that sentence sound derisive. Few would like having the holes in their plan pointed out by a young woman. Not Jacob. There was a smile in his voice, if not on his lips, and something else too. Pride?

"How do you bribe a ghost? He won't want financial gain."

He picked up my plate. "Eggs?"

"Very amusing."

"Truth is, I don't know. Fear? Curiosity? We'll think of something when we confront him." He set down the plate, his face suddenly dark and serious. "I should go. Arbuthnot stayed overnight at a pub at Victoria Dock. I'll go and see if he's still there. You fetch Culvert and meet me at The Three Knots. Do you know it?"

"I've seen it before."

"I'll allow you to come with us, but you will not be leaving the coach. Understand?" He disappeared without so much as a goodbye, probably so I wouldn't have a chance to protest.

I sighed and went to find Celia to tell her I was going to George's house for more research. She was in the small parlor entering figures into columns in the household ledger. A knock at the front door sounded before I could speak to her.

"I wonder who would be calling this early," she said. We removed ourselves to the bigger drawing room to receive our guest or guests.

Lucy came in a moment later, her cheeks pink and her eyes bright. "A Mr. Theodore Hyde to see you, Miss Emily."

I almost fell off my chair in shock.

CHAPTER 5

Theodore Hyde! I didn't get a chance to gather my wits because he was right behind Lucy. He bowed to me. "Thank you for receiving me so early, Miss Chambers."

"Oh, uh, of course. Mr. Hyde, may I present my sister, Miss Celia Chambers." He bowed again.

"Thank you, Lucy," Celia said. The maid turned her blush on Mr. Hyde, sighed then left very slowly, casting doe-eyed glances at Theodore over her shoulder as she did so.

Theodore wasn't smiling. Indeed, he looked very different from when I'd first met him. He was no longer jovial and friendly. Instead, he looked like a man in search of answers.

"I met Mr. Hyde at the Arbuthnots' house," I told Celia. "He's Mrs. Arbuthnot's nephew."

"Oh?" She smiled at him then at me, an unspoken question in her hopeful glance. I resisted the urge to roll my eyes. If I told her he was a poor relation of the Arbuthnots, would she stop her matchmaking? Probably not. Theodore might be poor by his aunt's standards, but I doubt he was poor by ours.

"Forgive me, Miss Chambers," he said. He cleared his throat. "But I want to know what happened to my cousin."

Celia and I glanced at each other.

"Please," he said. He leaned forward, his hat clasped loosely in front of his knees. "I know who you are, Miss Chambers. I know you're a spirit medium."

"Ah," Celia said. It seemed she was capable of speaking only single words of one syllable.

"And I suspect you are able to explain what happened to my cousin." He ran a hand through his thick blond hair. "He hasn't returned home, you see, and my aunt is very worried. She's taken to her bed and refuses to rise. She's convinced that the terrible business that befell Wallace's friend, Beaufort, has befallen him too."

"I assure you, it hasn't," I said.

His brows rose in surprise and he leaned back. "So you do know what's happened to him?"

Theodore had not looked at me differently when he admitted knowing I was a medium. There was no sneer on his face, no disdain in his voice, no hint that he didn't believe me. He simply stated a fact and now he wanted answers about his cousin. I saw no reason to keep the truth from him. I didn't think he would run screaming from the house in terror.

"He's been possessed."

He drew a breath. Two. "Well." He scratched his chin. "When I learned what you did for a living, I wondered if something like that had happened to Wallace." He fixed his gentle gray eyes on me. "Thank you for your honesty, Miss Chambers." His smile was grim.

"Rest assured my sister is doing everything she can to separate your cousin from the spirit inside him," Celia said. "She is quite a capable young woman."

"I don't doubt it."

"She's very resourceful for a seventeen year-old. Mature too, all of our acquaintance say so."

I groaned inwardly. "As my sister so subtly puts it, Mr. Hyde, I promise to do everything I can for your cousin. It won't be long before he's back home." Dear God, I hoped so.

"Surely you cannot do it on your own."

"Oh no," Celia said. "The ghost of Jacob Beaufort is helping."

He cocked his head to the side. "Wallace's friend? The one whose death you came to discuss when all this occurred?"

"The very one," I said.

"It sounds dangerous." He frowned. "I don't think the spirit possessing Wallace is a particularly friendly one. Are you sure Beaufort's help is enough?"

"It won't be dangerous for Emily," Celia said. The look she gave me was hard, challenging. "Mr. Beaufort's spirit will find your cousin, Mr. Hyde, and then all Emily need do is utter the final words to send the possessing spirit back. She won't be close to danger at all. Isn't that right, Em?"

"Quite. Indeed, I was just leaving to go to my friend George Culvert's house to..." I glanced at Celia. "...to research the incantation needed to oust the spirit." I didn't tell her Jacob had found Arbuthnot. If I did, she might not let me go. She would want Jacob to bring him here where she could maintain some control. That was an impossibility.

"May I come?" Theodore asked. "To help you with your research?" I began to shake my head, but he put his hand up. "Please, Miss Chambers. I need to do something useful and I don't particularly want to return to my aunt's home and tell her there's nothing to be done but wait."

I understood his dilemma perfectly. Waiting for others to do all the work was terribly frustrating. "Certainly. We could do with another set of eyes on the books."

The plan seemed to please Celia. Her grin could not have been wider. The prospect of me being alone with two eligible men made her positively giddy. I suspected, if she hadn't already begun planning my trousseau, she would now. "Mrs. Culvert will be there, will she not?" she asked.

"Of course. She's always at home." I doubted she knew I was lying, but the fact she never questioned me about

George's mother indicated she didn't want to know too much.

I gathered my cloak, hat, and gloves and left with Theodore Hyde at my side. It was a pleasant walk to George's house and we easily filled it with chatter. He told me about his home in Shropshire and made the countryside sound so picturesque that even I, a city-dweller through and through, wanted to see it by the time he finished.

He then asked me about my life as a medium. "How did you find out I was a medium?" I asked.

He looked at me sideways, a small smile twitching his lips. "I guessed. I didn't know for certain until you and your sister confirmed it just now."

"You tricked us!"

He winced. "It does seem that way, doesn't it? I didn't mean any harm, and I am sorry if I've caused offence." He nudged my elbow. "Forgive me?"

I nudged him back and smiled. "I suppose so."

"So what sort of research are we going to do at your friend's house?"

"Ah. Well. I lied about that to appease my sister. She's protective to the point of smothering."

"I understand that." He looked at me beneath hooded lids, his eyes smoky. My insides did a little flip. "So tell me, what is the real plan?" he asked.

"Jacob has found Wallace at a pub at the Victoria Dock."

He stopped and caught my shoulders. "Then we must go there! Now!"

"No, Mr. Hyde." I spoke with deliberate calm and withdrew his hands from my shoulders. I quickly dropped them because people were staring, and touching him made me feel uncomfortable, not afraid just...unsure. "We'll collect George then all three of us will travel there together in his coach. I suspect I'll have to remain in it while he and Jacob fetch Wallace out of the pub." I clicked my tongue. "I don't think they'll let me follow them inside, unfortunately."

"Quite rightly," he said.

Wonderful. Another overprotective person in my life. I already had Jacob and Celia, I didn't need more. Thank goodness George wasn't so restrictive. "You are welcome to stay in the coach with me."

He shook his head. "I'll go inside with them. Your friends might need me. Tell me," he said as we continued walking, "how does the spirit of Jacob Beaufort interact with live people?"

I told him all I knew about ghosts, the Waiting Area and the Otherworld. He seemed very interested and not at all afraid or bored.

We arrived at George's house in what felt like a very short time. I introduced George to Theodore as we waited for the coach to be brought around from the stables. I'd just finished when Jacob popped in, so I had to begin the introductions again, a difficult task considering Theodore couldn't see Jacob and Jacob scowled back at him.

"Why's he here?" he asked. He stood with his feet apart and arms crossed.

"Mr. Hyde is very concerned about his cousin," I said, keeping the irritation out of my voice for Theodore's sake. I didn't want him to know that Jacob had already made up his mind to dislike him.

Jacob grunted in response. "It's going to be crowded in the coach."

"Is Mr. Arbuthnot still at The Three Knots?" I asked.

He nodded as he circled around Theodore, assessing him. They were of a similar height and about the same size, but there the similarity ended. It was like looking at night and day, dark and light. The way Jacob sized him up made me uncomfortable and when I'm uncomfortable, I talk.

"I'll stay in the coach while you three go inside the pub and bring him out. Actually, now that we have Mr. Hyde to help George, you might not be needed, Jacob."

He stopped and looked at me. Just looked. The small muscles on either side of his jaw worked. I felt a little like a fly trapped in a spider's web, unable to move. My chest suddenly tightened and I remembered to breathe.

What had I said wrong? Why was he making me feel this way?

"Please call me Theo."

I must have turned a dumb-struck gaze on Theodore because he said, "You all seem to be on a first name basis with each other, so I want you to call me Theo."

"Certainly, Theo," George said cheerfully. He had no idea how heavy my heart felt.

"Miss Chambers, is everything all right?" Theo asked.

"Emily," George said, laughing. "First names, remember?"

"Emily?" Theo asked again.

"I'm well." I pressed a hand to my forehead. "Just a turn." I glanced at Jacob, but he no longer looked at me. He sat down on the arm of the sofa and lowered his head to his hands.

I went to him and reached out to press my hand to the back of his neck. But I didn't touch him.

"Ah, there's the coach," George said. "Shall we?"

I looked up, straight into the soft gray eyes of Theo. He gave me a crooked smile and held out his elbow for me to take.

I did. When I glanced over my shoulder, Jacob was gone.

***

I thought I wouldn't see Jacob until we reached our destination, but he reappeared in the coach. Whatever emotions had overcome him in George's drawing room were replaced with a business-like manner.

"When we get to the Three Knots, you'll wait in the coach," he said. "The footmen and driver will remain behind and George is to give them instructions not to leave you. George, Theo, and I will go inside and bring Arbuthnot out to you. Now, let's go through the words you need to use to send the spirit back."

I spent the rest of the journey memorizing what I had to say. I shivered when I first heard the incantation. It was so like that other time when we had fought the demon. In fact, the similarity was too close for my liking—as if the same hand was behind both.

But we had killed Finch, the man controlling the shape-shifting demon, and banished his accomplice, Mr. Blunt. Jacob had terrified Blunt—the master of the North London School for Domestic Service—so much that he'd left the city in a hurry. We had been quite certain, however, that Blunt didn't have the capacity to be the architect of the scheme.

We may have been wrong.

If Jacob and George felt the similarity too, they didn't say.

The Victoria Docks wasn't a dangerous place, or no more so than any other busy London hub in the middle of the morning. And it was certainly busy! Noise hummed all around—the whir of cranes stretching into the sky like fingers, the hammering of builders at the eastern end, the rumble of cart wheels, the shouts from dock-workers loading and unloading, and the clack of crates being stacked one on top of the other. Foremen, carters, porters, merchants, and sailors milled together with passengers of all shapes, sizes and colors. I counted at least four different languages as people walked past the coach's open window. Over their heads I saw the rigging of moored ships forming intricate webs between masts. In the distance, a train whistle blew.

"There's the Three Knots," Jacob said. He indicated a crooked building of three levels leaning drunkenly on its neighbor, a warehouse. "Tell the driver to wait in that street there. It's narrow, but it leads to Prince Regent Lane. So many of these small streets go nowhere and I don't want you to be caught in one of them."

His good advice hung in the air between us. My safety was always at the forefront of his mind. It had not always been so. Once, he thought my life ending would be a good thing because it would bring us together. It seemed he no longer thought that.

I touched his hand resting on the seat between us, and he

curled his fingers around mine. Then he let go and was gone. He reappeared on the outside of the coach.

I gave George and Theo the instructions from Jacob. George blew out a breath, slow and measured, and pushed his spectacles up his nose. "Tell Beaufort he owes me a large brandy after this."

On impulse I leaned forward and squeezed his hand as I had done to Jacob. George smiled grimly and squeezed back. I glanced out the window and saw Jacob eyeing our linked hands, his eyes hooded, his expression masked. I let go and wondered what he'd have done if it was Theo's hand I touched.

George and Theo alighted from the carriage and George gave the footmen, two of his biggest and burliest, instructions not to leave me. Then the two men and one ghost strode to the Three Knots with purposeful strides. I felt a swell of pride as I watched them.

I had never been very patient, but waiting for them to reappear set my nerves on edge. I sat on one seat then switched to the other side, then back again. To pass the time, I counted the number of women wearing blue mantles—six—and the number of times a train whistle blew—eight—and their frequency—every minute. I untied my bonnet. I retied my bonnet. I would have counted the money in my reticule, but I already knew it contained only three shillings. I counted twelve men and two women entering the Three Knots and six men and one girl leave.

The girl!

She had dark springy hair and was aged about ten. She was looking down, so I couldn't see her face, but I knew it was the same one who'd summoned the spirit. She walked beside a figure cloaked in black wearing a wide hat, his face also cast down. They hurried quickly away.

I put a hand to the door handle but hesitated. I'd been ordered to remain in the coach. George and Theo would be angry with me for leaving. Jacob would be furious.

But the girl and her accomplice were getting away! Soon

they would be entirely gone from view, consumed by the shadows cast by the many tall warehouses.

I looked to The Three Knots. I could summon Jacob but decided against it. George and Theo may be confronting the spirit right now and they needed Jacob more than me.

The girl and the black-cloaked man were almost at the corner of the furthest warehouse. I had to go. My friends had a job to do and so did I, one that didn't involve communicating with a ghost. I was more than merely a conduit to the dead.

I opened the coach door and jumped down. "Miss?" one of the footmen called down from the rumble seat at the back. "Everything all right?"

Just then, the door to The Three Knots opened, crashing back on its hinges. Wallace Arbuthnot barreled out, his red cheeks puffing hard. He paused, looked around and spotted me. A twisted grin split his fleshy face.

I gasped and clambered back inside the cabin, snagging my skirt on the corner of the coach step. I snapped it free.

"Miss?" the footman said again. I felt the coach rock as he stepped down and I leaned out of the open door to tell him to stop Wallace Arbuthnot.

It was too late. Arbuthnot was faster than he looked, and a large man traveling at speed is a force not to be trifled with. He shouldered the footman out of the way and dove into the cabin, landing on the seat beside me.

I might have emitted a small scream—very well, a large one—and slid across the seat into the far corner. Not far enough. Arbuthnot grinned that horrible grin again. "Good. Entertainment for the journey." He punched the roof of the cabin. "Drive on!" he shouted.

Silence.

"Miss?" The panicky voice of the footman came from near the door. I couldn't see him past Arbuthnot's massive frame.

I opened my mouth to warn him, but Wallace moved fast. All of a sudden something cold and sharp pressed against my throat. A blade. Arbuthnot's breath, reeking of ale and tobacco, was hot on my cheek.

"Drive on," he snarled, "or I gut her."

I tried to lean away from the knife, but Arbuthnot—or rather, the spirit possessing him—grabbed the back of my hair and held me against his reeking, filthy body. I winced but remained silent. I dared not make a sound, dared not breathe.

"Move this growler now, or I rip her apart!" he shouted again.

The coach rolled forward and the vein in my neck throbbed against the cold metal. An unladylike drop of moisture trickled down my spine. I closed my eyes to block out Arbuthnot's wild glare and tried to still my racing heartbeat. *Calm. Be calm. Think.*

"Faster!" he roared over the *clip clop* of hooves and the rumble of wheels. "Get me to Victoria Station, you dog, or this pretty neck gets sliced!"

The coach sped up. I wondered if the other footman was still on board, or if he too had jumped off to alert George. Of course he wouldn't be much use in rescuing me but Jacob might, or Theo.

Arbuthnot circled his arm around my shoulders. He hooked the knife under my chin and pressed his thigh against mine. He stank and his white shirt and silk waistcoat were stained beyond repair. The real Wallace Arbuthnot would be appalled. The possessed one pushed the blade harder into the skin beneath my chin and chuckled when I cried out.

"Very pretty neck." His voice, while essentially the same as Arbuthnot's, sounded quite different. More raw somehow, and heavy with drink. He laughed again. Then he licked me below the earlobe. Everything inside me constricted into a tight ball, but on the outside I remained passive. At least, I hoped that's how I appeared.

I dug my fingers into the leather of the seat. "Mr. Arbuthnot," I whispered. "Wallace, can you hear me?"

"Shut it!"

I steeled myself and tried again. "Mr. Arbuthnot, fight him. Please, Mr. Arbuthnot." I yelped as the knife bit into my flesh.

"My name is Mortlock. Jim Mortlock."

I shivered at the cold, dead tone. He must have felt it because he said, "You're afraid of me, ain't you? You should be. Some of the things I done when I was alive would make you sick. Things a good little girl like you never hears about. Bad things. Wicked." His throaty chuckle made my scalp crawl. I didn't want to hear his story, but I had to. Knowing more about the spirit might reveal something about the people who'd summoned him and why.

"Tell me," I whispered. "I want to know."

That horrible laugh again. "When I died, they said 'good riddance.' Said I got no conscience to do the things I done. I'm good with a knife, see." He stroked the blade down my throat to my collar and dipped the point inside the bodice. I tensed and squeezed my eyes shut. "Decorated my Ma with a blade just like this one. Drew a pretty pattern from here," he pressed the point against one ear, "to here." The cool metal traced across my throat to my other ear, not hard enough to pierce the skin, but it may have left a red mark. I prayed the coach didn't go over any bumps.

"Why are you here now?" I asked. "What do you want?"

"I want some fun." He licked my throat near the knife point. Bile rose and I gagged. That produced another rasping chuckle from Mortlock. "I'm legend, see. They remember me after I'm gone as the one with no conscience. That man and that girl, they called me here and I came. Better than Hell or whatever's waiting for me beyond."

He meant beyond the Waiting Area. All ghosts ended up there after death. Some remained until they'd resolved any issues they'd left behind. Others moved on quickly. Where they went depended on how they'd behaved in life. Jim Mortlock probably wasn't going to a peaceful resting place.

I swallowed my fear and forged on. "Why did they want

you?" I asked. "What's your purpose here?"

"Talkative little bitch, eh?" He snorted in my ear. "He wants those toffs to suffer like he did."

"Which toffs?" But I knew. I knew.

"That lord and lady and their girl. He wanted to humiliate them, make their boy watch as his sister did some awful bad things because of me."

Oh God, oh God. Someone had done that to Adelaide deliberately? But who? Why?

I didn't have to think hard for an answer. Whoever had killed Jacob out of revenge was now taking it further by putting his family through further misery. The one who'd released the shape-shifting demon had also summoned Mortlock into Adelaide's body.

"Too bad I didn't want to stay in the girl." I could hear him grin in my ear. "Oh, I liked what I saw in the mirror. Had a nice time that night alone in her room." His hand gripped one of my breasts and squeezed. He grunted, perhaps in disappointment that he didn't get a handful, and let go. His fingers trailed down my ribcage to my waist.

"But you didn't want to be in a woman's body?" I asked quickly. A moment or two more and I would call Jacob, but first I wanted to learn all I could from Mortlock.

His hand stilled and his palm flattened against my stomach. "Nope. Didn't want no footman's body neither. No better than scum, they are. I wanted to be the master. This body was the best on offer so I took it."

"Do they know? The people who summoned you here? Do they know you transferred to Mr. Arbuthnot's body?"

"They do now. Must have worked it out."

"Did they ask you to do their bidding, whatever that is?"

He snorted. "I do no man's bidding. No girl's neither." His hand dipped to my skirt and he pressed himself into my side. I kept my gaze fixed on the opposite wall. "I eat pretty girls for breakfast."

Just one more question. One more. "What does he look like? The man who summoned you with the little girl?"

"No more talking," he growled. "We're nearly at the station and I want my entertainment." Faster than a blink, he flipped up my skirt and pinched my thigh through my stocking.

I gasped and tried to shove him away, but he was too big, too strong, and he held the knife against my thigh. He sneered and a chill seeped into my bones. He was going to cut me, or have his way with me, or both.

And when he'd finished, he'd kill me.

CHAPTER 6

"Jacob!" His name was barely out of my mouth when he came. Cold fury deadened his eyes as he took in the scene. He looked around for a weapon since he couldn't use his fists on a live body. If we could draw Mortlock out of Arbuthnot, that would be a different matter. Spirits could interact with other spirits.

"Knife," I said to Jacob, but he'd already seen it.

"You want it, eh?" Mortlock grinned, but it was wiped off his face when Jacob grabbed the blade. Confused, Mortlock glanced up and around, but he held onto the weapon so they performed a tug-of-war over it. The knife would have sliced mortal flesh to pieces, but Jacob could not feel pain or bleed anymore. "What are you doing, witch? Stop it, or I'll gut you."

With Mortlock occupied and off-balance, I did what Jacob couldn't do. I pushed the big body of Wallace Arbuthnot off me. But in an attempt to steady himself, Mortlock pushed hard on the knife. Jacob couldn't hold onto it. The knife cut my thigh.

I screamed as my flesh tore open. The coach came to a hard stop. I rocked and Mortlock fell forward. Jacob snatched the knife off him.

"Emily!" He was at my side in a heartbeat.

The door opened a mere inch and the wild-eyed driver peeped cautiously inside. With a grunt, Mortlock pushed the door open all the way and the driver tumbled back to the road. Both men swore.

"Jacob, stop him! He's getting away!"

He shook his head. "You're bleeding. Take off your cloak."

"But Jacob!"

"I'm staying here with you. Tell the driver to chase him."

I gave the order and the driver took off in the direction of Mortlock, but the villain had already been swallowed up by the crowd of passengers outside Victoria Station and I doubted the driver would have any luck.

"Your cloak," Jacob prompted without taking his gaze off the bloodied slash.

With my skirts still bunched up, I was revealing a lot of thigh as well as the wound. The heat of his gaze warmed me all over and I should have felt ashamed, but I didn't. Perhaps it was because he was a ghost, or perhaps it was simply because he was Jacob, *my* Jacob, I didn't mind the way he looked at me—as if he wanted to kiss me there. I *wanted* him to kiss my thigh.

I removed my cloak and handed it to him. He put the knife on the floor beside his knee and dabbed the wound near the garter. It stung a little and I sucked air between my teeth.

He eased back. "Emily?" The quaver in his voice concerned me more than the cut.

"It's all right," I said. "It's just a scratch."

He inspected the wound. "It's more than a scratch." His free hand cupped my thigh and his thumb caressed my skin through the torn stocking. I sighed and relaxed. He dabbed at the blood with the cloak some more. It had stopped bleeding and we could now inspect the damage.

"My stocking is ruined," I said, trying to be light.

He said nothing. His thumb continued to stroke my

thigh. I couldn't see his face, intent as he was on the wound.

"I'd better hide it from my sister," I went on.

Still he said nothing. He bent his head forward and I thought he would kiss my knee, but instead he rested his forehead there. He heaved a deep, body-shuddering sigh and gently grasped my calf.

I stroked his hair until he composed himself.

"Tend to this when you get home," he said, voice shaky. He drew my skirts down over my legs but remained kneeling at my feet.

"I'll try."

"Try?" He looked up. His face was blanched. Not white, as there was no blood in him to drain away, but pinched and drawn. He looked older.

"I don't want to alarm Celia," I said. "Asking for salves and bandages might alert her to something being amiss."

"I'll get anything you need." He sat on the seat opposite me and leaned forward, resting his elbows on his knees. He looked exhausted, although not even that was possible for a ghost.

The driver returned. "Slippery as an eel, that one," he said with a shake of his head. "Sorry, miss. I alerted a constable but..." He shrugged.

"It's all right. We'd better return to Victoria Dock and retrieve the others."

He tugged his forelock, having lost his hat, and climbed up to the box. The coach rolled on.

"They are still at the dock, aren't they?" I asked.

Jacob nodded. "We were at The Three Knots when I heard your summoning." I wasn't sure if calling out his name once could count as a summoning, but I said nothing. "George and Theo were asking around about Arbuthnot when the footmen came in and told us you'd been..." His eyelids lowered and remained closed for a few long seconds. "I darted around looking for you, but...there are a lot of black coaches in the area." He rubbed his hand over his eyes and when he removed it, a light that hadn't been there before shone in them. "Why didn't you call me earlier? You know I can't locate you until you do."

"I wanted to get some answers from him first."

"Jesus, Emily!" His outburst startled me and my nerves, already frayed, jumped. He sat back, folded his arms over his chest, unfolded them and re-folded them. "My apologies," he muttered. "But having a conversation with mad spirits is a very stupid thing to do."

"I got some useful information," I said, indignant.

The look he focused on me was sharper than the blade still lying on the cabin floor. "You should have called me immediately."

I sighed. "You would have alerted him to your presence somehow and then he wouldn't have said anything."

"I don't bloody care, Emily. Never, *ever* do something like that again. Understand? Otherwise I'll have to haunt you forever for your own sake."

I quite liked the sound of that. The way his gaze softened and he quickly looked away told me he realized his threat was pointless.

"If I was capable of aging," he said quietly, "I would look about fifty right now."

For some reason I found that funny and I laughed. He didn't join in and stared out the window. His jaw formed a rigid line in profile, his lips pressed tightly together. Neither of us spoke the rest of the way back to the Three Knots.

***

Once George and Theo joined us, my silence didn't last long. I told them everything Mortlock had told me, including his suggestion that the Beauforts were being targeted by the girl and the person with her, and my idea that it was the same villain who'd released the demon.

Jacob swore and punched the side of the cabin. George jumped, but Theo merely raised his eyebrows then nodded in understanding.

"We'll warn your family," Theo said. Not knowing how tall Jacob was, he spoke to Jacob's chest rather than his face.

"Don't worry. No harm will come to anyone."

We all knew we couldn't guarantee their safety. Without knowing who was behind the summoning, we might as well have been blindfolded. What was to stop the girl and her accomplice calling another spirit? What was to stop them going to the Belgravia house and firing a pistol?

But something told me our villain was playing a more subtle, supernatural game.

"I'll warn Lady Preston, just in case," I added.

"I'll do it," George said. "I can stop by on my way home."

"I'm not sure your ways are delicate enough, George."

He pouted. "I'm good at being delicate where ladies are concerned."

Jacob rolled his eyes. I tried not to laugh, since it wasn't a laughing matter. I didn't want Lady Preston or Adelaide to worry, but I did want them to be alert until Mortlock was safely back in the Waiting Area and the people who'd summoned him had been dealt with.

"Of course you are," I said to George. "But even so, I'd like to come along. Shall we go now?"

"Can you drop me home first?" Theo said. "As much as I'd like to join you, I must check on my aunt. I left her in a bit of a state this morning."

Jacob seemed to brighten at this.

"As you wish," George said. He pulled down the window and shouted instructions to the driver.

The gentle rocking of the coach would have been soothing if my mind wasn't in turmoil and my leg didn't throb. I watched Jacob sitting in the corner like a dark thunder cloud. He seemed in no mood for talking.

"We must find Mortlock," I said. "Before he does something awful."

George removed his hat and wiped his brow. "But how?"

"I'll repeat my search," Jacob said, "starting immediately after you're home safe."

"Jacob will find him," I told George.

"Of course, of course," he muttered.

Theo nodded. "We must also find the girl who summoned the spirit, and the man with her. For the Beauforts' safety."

"He must think we're all stupid," Jacob mumbled.

I tried to ignore him, but I wasn't very good at it. Ignoring Jacob was like ignoring my arms and legs. He was so much a part of me.

"I think the girl and her friend knew Mortlock when he was alive," he added.

I stared at him then repeated what he'd said for George and Theo's benefit.

"Of course," George said. "Otherwise how would they know whom to summon?"

I rubbed my eyes with my thumb and forefinger. He was right. It made sense.

Theo agreed. "So find out more about Mortlock and we might find out more about the people behind the summoning."

"There's another way we can learn about them." I took a deep breath and repeated everything Celia had told me about my father and how I suspected the girl was his daughter too, and therefore my sister. I told them about Louis' father's shop and that we might discover where he lived if we asked the current owner, Mr. Graves. We might find the girl through him.

I steeled myself for their reaction to my scandalous origins. I was a bastard, a child born out of wedlock with African blood. I wasn't sure what to expect from the men who belonged to the class of privilege and propriety. Scorn? Pity? Disgust?

Certainly not the smile I received from Jacob, the first real one I'd seen on his face for some time. "This is good, Emily," he said. "When the business with Mortlock is over, you can begin your search for your father. If he hasn't returned then I can look for him in New South Wales, if I can go there." Jacob was not the usual sort of ghost. Most spirits were tied to the location where they'd died, if they chose to remain in this realm at all—unless they possessed a living person, that is. Jacob could go anywhere he wanted in spirit form. He also looked solid to me and as alive as George and Theo, whereas other ghosts appeared faded, their edges smudged like a charcoal drawing. I didn't think New South Wales would prove a great challenge for my ghost.

Louis might no longer be there anyway. The existence of the girl would suggest he'd returned to England long enough to father her. If she was indeed his daughter too—she might be from an entirely different branch of our family tree.

Jacob seemed to sense my reservations. He leaned forward and touched my knee. "Don't be afraid."

I nodded but said nothing lest I begin to cry. His determination touched my aching heart.

"So your father was a grocer's son?" George said. I waited for the snobbish curl of his lip. It didn't come. "Then to Mr. Graves the grocer's we shall go, after we deposit Theo and visit Lady Preston."

***

It was only a short journey from Kensington to Belgravia. According to the stiff butler who greeted us at the front door, Lady Preston and Adelaide were at home. Unfortunately so was Lord Preston. He must have heard our voices because he emerged from the library adjoining the entrance hall with a fierce expression.

"Good day, my lord," George said, bowing.

Lord Preston didn't acknowledge him, didn't even look at him. "Get out of my house, Miss Chambers," he snarled. "Or Polson here will throw you out."

Jacob stalked up to his father and stood chest to chest with him. They were the same height, but Lord Preston's build was heavier and his bushy eyebrows and thick-set jaw gave him a more menacing demeanor. I trembled. I wouldn't put it past him to pick me up and throw me bodily onto the street himself.

"If I were alive..." Jacob didn't finish the sentence. He moved away and stood near the hall table. His finger rubbed the rim of the silver salver in a deceptively lazy gesture.

I shook my head slightly and silently willed him not to pick it up. Lord Preston had accused me of using trickery before when in fact it was Jacob's ghost wielding objects. I didn't want to go through that ordeal again.

"We'd like to see Lady Preston," I said.

"Polson, see Miss Chambers out. Her friend too."

"George Culvert," George said, extending his hand. Bless him for trying to maintain a semblance of civility.

Lord Preston ignored it. "Never heard of you."

George's fingers curled. He cleared his throat. "Uh, we, er..."

"We've come to alert you to a danger," I said. Lord Preston was an obstacle we weren't going to get past, but I was determined to warn him anyway. My conscience wouldn't allow me to walk away, not from Adelaide and Lady Preston. "Someone could be trying to harm your family—"

"The only person doing harm to this family is you, Miss Chambers. Now get out. Polson!"

"Father?" Adelaide appeared at the top of the sweeping staircase. "What— Oh, Miss Chambers."

Beside me, I could hear George gasp. "Introduce me," he whispered.

"Miss Beaufort, may I present my friend, George Culvert. He knew Jacob at Eton."

"Is no one here listening to me?" Lord Preston bellowed.

Adelaide descended the stairs, a vision of loveliness in a cream silk day dress with black lace at the elbows and a double row of black buttons down the bodice. "Very pleased to meet you, Mr. Culvert." She smiled at him and offered her hand.

He didn't take it first but simply stared at her, open-mouthed. Eventually he remembered his manners and bowed deeply over her hand.

"I didn't know Beaufort's sister was so...grown up," George said, beaming at her.

"Bloody hell," Jacob muttered. "He's spoken two words to her and thinks he's in love already."

I didn't tell him that it took me less than that to realize I loved him.

I glanced from Adelaide to George and smiled. At least George would no longer try to court me now.

"Is Jacob here?" Adelaide asked, looking around.

"Enough!" Lord Preston snapped. "Do not encourage this charlatan."

"Father, Mother and I believe she is a true medium."

Lord Preston snorted, turned and strode to the door. He opened it himself and stood aside. "Leave."

Jacob lifted the silver salver but fortunately lowered it before anyone saw.

Adelaide went to her father and put a hand on his arm. "Please let them stay. Mother may like to hear what Miss Chambers has to say."

"Your mother needs rest. Her mind has been weakened by...events. The last thing she needs is to listen to these people." He opened the door wider.

She turned to me and sighed.

"It's all right." I glanced at Lord Preston. His thick brow was drawn and the large lips formed a severe line beneath his gray moustache. I had only a moment, and I took it. "I came to warn you to stay indoors if possible. We think someone is trying to bring harm to your family."

Adelaide gasped. Lord Preston repeated his order for us to leave. I held up my hands in surrender and strode past him out the door. When I realized neither George nor Jacob followed me, I stopped. George had hold of Adelaide's hand in both of his and was patting it. He said something to her, but I couldn't hear what. He let go and came after me. Jacob remained behind, glaring daggers at his father. Lord Preston shut the door.

"I dislike that man intensely," I said, climbing into

George's coach. I sat back in the seat with a sigh and pressed my fingers into my eyes. Lord Preston was an exhausting man.

George instructed the driver to travel to Chelsea's High Street, then he climbed in opposite me and the footman closed the door. "She is quite lovely," George said. "Beaufort, do you think your parents would allow me to court her?"

"He's not here," I said. The coach rolled forward and I looked out at the row of houses, like pretty, fresh debutantes lined up for inspection. "And if you'll allow me to answer you, the answer is no. You are now associated with me, and Lord Preston hates me."

The light in George's eyes went out. "I dislike that man too."

Jacob joined us in the coach when we stopped in front of Mr. Graves's fruit and vegetable shop. I alerted George then asked Jacob if he'd done anything foolish at his parents' house.

He shook his head, but I wasn't sure if I believed him. His mood certainly hadn't lifted. I could feel vibrations of anger coming off him. He said nothing and I didn't question him further.

Unfortunately Mr. Graves didn't know anything about the previous owner of his grocery shop except that he was a "darky," had an accent and his name was "Fran-swars Something-Foreign." He couldn't tell us where he lived or anything about a young girl who might be his granddaughter. Mr. Graves had taken over the shop some fifteen years earlier, well before she'd been born.

We left there in a cloud of gloom and nobody spoke all the way to my house. The three of us parted at my door after assigning ourselves tasks. Jacob's task was to find Mortlock, mine was to ask Celia if there was anything else about Fran-Swars Something-Foreign she wasn't telling me, and George's task was to go home. If his slumped shoulders were any indication, he wasn't particularly happy to not be given a job to do.

That evening, after tending to my wound without alerting my sister or Lucy, I decided to accost Celia over dinner. She was less likely to walk away since manners dictated she remain until we'd both finished eating. "Celia, I have some more questions about my father's family. They must—"

"Enough, Emily!" Her knife and fork dropped onto the plate with a loud clank. "No more questions. I've told you all I know. Truly I have. Do you think I would withhold something important from you?"

"You withheld some very important information from me for seventeen years," I said acidly. "Such as the name of my father."

She tilted her chin at me. "There are lives at stake now. After what you just told me about this Mortlock spirit, I would not keep something vital from you if it related to the girl. It's imperative Mr. Culvert and Mr. Beaufort find her and stop her, and I am not *that* heartless that I wouldn't help if I could."

"I suppose not. Sorry, Celia." I didn't correct her and say that I would be helping Jacob and George. There was no need to add more kindling to an already smoldering fire.

Celia made a small miffed sound, picked up her knife and fork, and cut into her potato. She then proceeded to chat about her day. I tuned out when she got to her conversation with Mrs. Northrop about our neighbor's rusty door hinge.

***

Jacob didn't come to me the next morning. George, however, did.

"Remember our friend, Leviticus Price?" he asked with great excitement as he sat in our drawing room. Celia had gone out. I think she was avoiding me.

"I remember him." I screwed up my nose. Leviticus Price was a member of The Society For Supernatural Activity along with George, a group devoted to the discussion of all things supernatural. He'd helped us pinpoint Blunt and Finch as the persons behind the shape-shifting demon's escape from the Otherworld. I'd found him to be extremely disagreeable, and I didn't like him. "Why?"

"I think we should visit him again."

"You think he can help?"

"Well." He crossed his legs and fixed me with an earnest stare. "I started thinking about your suggestion, that this situation is related to the one we had with the demon, and the possibility that the culprit is the same. Price is a board member at the school where Blunt worked. Perhaps he knows where he went, if indeed he went anywhere. Price is also well respected at the Society and extremely knowledgeable. He might know of another one such as yourself."

"The girl," I muttered.

He shrugged. "It's the only suggestion I have for now. Have you heard from Beaufort?"

"No." I sighed. "Shall we go?" I wanted to leave before Celia came home. The less I had to explain to her the better.

I tugged on the bell pull and Lucy met me at the drawing room door a moment later. "I'm going to Mr. Culvert's house to study his books." The ease with which I lied lately was alarming. I told myself I was protecting Celia from worry. I almost believed it.

Lucy fetched my coat, gloves and hat, and saw us out. I climbed into George's coach and waited until we were on our way before I asked him the question on my mind.

"Why did you come here to fetch me? Did you not want to see Price on your own?"

He chuckled. "I'm not as cowardly as that, Emily."

My face heated. "I'm sorry. That's not what I meant. I'm simply unsure why I'm needed."

"I thought you might like to come along."

"I would, but I don't think you asked me out of politeness. Visiting Leviticus Price is not a fun outing."

He grinned. "He liked you."

"He did not."

"He did. You impressed him, not only with your ability to

see ghosts, but your manner. You weren't afraid of him."

"I was."

"But you didn't show it and that is even more impressive." He cleared his throat and looked out the window. "Adelaide Beaufort stood up to her father yesterday. She's another impressive young lady." His cheeks colored and he pushed his glasses up his nose.

We spent the journey to Price's house talking about Adelaide. At least, George talked and I mostly listened. Sometimes I didn't even do that.

Price rented rooms in a modest brick house situated in the middle of a long street in a new suburb. There were no trees, no common greens, and only one house had a cheerful window box of red flowers. The rest could have been unoccupied for all their blandness.

George knocked on the front door of Price's house. No one came. He knocked again. Finally the door opened on Price's landlady, a middle-aged woman with graying hair and protruding nose, chin and mouth. It was as if her maker had stroked and teased the bottom half of her face to stretch it. She tied the strings of an apron behind her back without taking her hard gaze off us.

"He's not home," she said when George asked to see Price. She spoke with an accent I couldn't place.

"Oh," I said, disappointed. "Are you sure?"

"Course I'm sure. He's not here." She crossed her arms, blocking our entry with her bulk.

"Mrs....?"

"None of your business."

Well! How rude! Her reception was most unexpected. What had we done to her? Or to Price for that matter?

"Nevermind, George." I took his arm. "There's another way to find out about Blunt."

He tipped his hat to Mrs. None-of-your-business and walked with me to the coach. Before I climbed in, I glanced up at the second floor window. The curtain fluttered closed but not before I saw the white hair and long face of Price.

CHAPTER 7

"Clerkenwell," I said to the driver before climbing into the coach. "The North London School for Domestic Service." He knew where it was as he'd driven us there before.

George nodded. "Good idea. Mrs. White might know where Blunt has gone." We settled on opposite seats in the cabin and the footman folded up the step and closed the door. "It's a shame Price wouldn't talk to us," George said as the coach pulled out of the street. He must have seen the face at the window too. "I was hoping he'd know something about possession." He shrugged one shoulder. "We must have caught him at an awkward time."

I wondered if that awkward time had anything to do with the landlady tying up her apron. Her hair had been a little too disheveled for the middle of the morning and the top button of her dress was undone. I suspected she and Price were more than merely landlady and tenant.

Not that I would tell George. There are some things that friends of the opposite sex should not discuss.

"Where are you going?" Jacob said upon appearing beside me. He sat as far away from me as possible. I didn't move to give him more room.

"Jacob's here," I said for George's benefit. I then

proceeded to tell Jacob about our reception at Price's and our plan to question Mrs. White about Blunt's whereabouts.

He frowned. "It's a good idea. We need to do something before..." He lowered his head and his shoulders slumped forward, deflated.

I touched his shoulder. He tensed. "What did you learn overnight?"

Jacob straightened. There was no trace of worry on his face. There was no trace of any emotions whatsoever. It was as if he'd shut down, closed off. "Mortlock is very dangerous. When he was alive he murdered three people, including his own mother."

I pressed a hand to my suddenly roiling stomach and relayed what he'd said to George. He gasped and muttered, "Good lord."

"The other two people he murdered were boys of about fifteen years."

It got worse and worse. "That's awful."

"They went to Blunt's Clerkenwell school and were known to Finch," Jacob said.

I gaped at him. Finch had been the young man controlling the shape-shifting demon. He'd been a pupil at the North London School for Domestic Service but was ordered to leave because he was too disruptive and not suitable for service. We'd killed him, but not before discovering Blunt, the school's master, had helped him.

"The murdered boys left the school around the same time as Finch and probably worked for his thieving operation. The Administrators and other spirits I questioned in the Waiting Area say Mortlock was one of their number, living in the slums, robbing whomever he could, and coercing those weaker than himself into paying protection money. He doesn't appear to have been a student at the school although the records may have been destroyed."

"You checked them?"

He nodded. "Mortlock died only last week."

"Last week?" I said.

"The day after Finch died and we sent the demon back."

I informed George and we all considered that for a few moments.

"I don't like this, Emily," Jacob said. "It's very dangerous. I want you to go home. Let George and I question Mrs. White about Blunt."

I turned to him fully and touched his cheek. I expected him to flinch, but he merely closed his eyes. "No," I said. "I will not go home when there is more I can do."

His eyes flew open and he caught my wrist. His grip was hard but not bruising. "Emily!"

The coach slowed and then stopped. We had arrived at the school. Clerkenwell was one of the better slum areas if such a thing existed. It was working class and poverty was rife as were all the things that went hand-in-hand with it— thieves, orphans, and hunger. The school offered refuge to those children with no other prospects except the workhouse or falling in with disreputable adults. It provided them with food, shelter, and an education in the domestic arts, which gave them a chance of finding work when they turned sixteen. Lucy our maid had been a student, as had some of George's staff.

"I think I shall become a patron," he said, stepping out of the coach behind me.

All three of us looked up at the school. Its bricks might be blackened by years of soot, but it was sturdy compared to the other buildings in the narrow street. It looked like it was holding up the tall, rickety houses on either side. If it was removed, they might all collapse into the vacant space, one on top of the other.

"What a worthy idea," I said. I knew George was wealthy as he didn't work, but I didn't know how wealthy. Obviously he had enough money to give to the school.

He knocked and a maid opened the door. "Is Mrs. White in?" George asked.

The maid shook her head. "Mrs. White has moved on, sir."

"Moved on?" I echoed. "When?"

"Few days ago, miss. Do you want to see Mr. Hollowbrooke, the new master?"

"Yes, thank you," said George.

Jacob disappeared as the maid led us into the drawing room, a large but barren and uncomfortable space containing only a desk and two hard guest chairs. We waited until she left before speaking.

"Beaufort still here?" George asked me.

I shook my head. "I can't believe Mrs. White has left."

"I know. I thought she loved this school."

We both contemplated the significance of that in silence until Mr. Hollowbrooke arrived. Jacob followed behind him. I raised my eyebrows in question, but he merely shrugged.

After the necessary introductions, George said, "We were hoping to find Mrs. White here, but it seems she has left. Such a great loss."

"Indeed." Mr. Hollowbrooke spoke as blandly as he looked, and he looked very bland. Brown hair, hazel eyes, neither short nor tall, fat nor thin. His age was indeterminate, his features common, unmarked and expressionless. He was someone you forgot soon after you've met him. Lucky Mr. Hollowbrooke. To go about unnoticed, without inquisitive and sometimes rude stares following your every move, must be liberating. A part of me did think it rather sad, but only a small part.

"We wanted to thank her for all she did for us," George said. "She has matched some wonderful servants to my household and to that of Miss Chambers."

A small wrinkle fought its way onto Mr. Hollowbrooke's flat forehead. "You're not here for another servant, Mr. Culvert?"

"No. Just to thank Mrs. White."

"Oh. Pity." He had not sat down and now he inched back toward the door. We were dismissed.

"Find out where she went," Jacob said.

"We would like to write to her and thank her," I said to

Mr. Hollowbrooke. "Do you have an address?"

"I'm afraid not," Mr. Hollowbrooke intoned. "She didn't leave one."

"Oh?" I said at the same time George asked, "Really?"

Jacob frowned. "Very odd."

"Did she get an appointment at another school perhaps?" I persisted. She could not simply have left without a trace.

"Not that I am aware of."

"What about Mr. Blunt, the previous master?" George asked. "Can you tell us where he is now?"

"No." Hollowbrooke pulled his watch out of his waistcoat pocket and checked the time. "Now unless there's anything else... I'm very busy..."

"Yes, of course," George said. "Thank you, Mr. Hollowbrooke."

Hollowbrooke left and the maid reappeared. She walked us to the front door.

"Do you know where Mrs. White or Mr. Blunt have gone?" I asked her. "We would dearly like to thank them both for finding us suitable maids. They were very helpful."

"I don't know where Mr. Blunt went," she said, rubbing her arms as if she were cold. "He just got up and left in the middle of the night last week. Very odd." She dropped her arms and smiled. No, beamed. I think she was very happy that Blunt had gone. I wasn't surprised, considering what he used to do in the girl's dormitory at night. "Mrs. White went a few days later. She said she needed to look after her sister who'd taken ill suddenly. Sad to see her go. Very sad." She sighed and opened the door.

"Do you know where her sister lives?" I asked.

"No, miss. Sorry, miss."

George took my arm and we stepped down the stairs to the waiting coach. Jacob followed. A group of children were inspecting the horses and the gold Culvert escutcheon painted on the door. The driver had hopped down and showed them how to pat the horses correctly but the stiff footmen had not moved from their perch. They both scowled as if assessing the number of grubby fingerprints on the glossy black paintwork.

"I'm going to check Hollowbrooke's office," Jacob said then disappeared.

George helped me up into the coach. "Well? What do you think?"

"I think someone is lying," I said. "Mrs. White didn't have any family."

"So she told us."

"Do you think that was a falsehood?" I asked. "Or is Hollowbrooke the one who invented the sister?"

He removed his glasses and rubbed the back of his hand across his forehead. "I don't know. Perhaps. He was certainly a difficult man to read."

I nodded. "Whoever is lying, they managed to convince the maid about the sister."

"Not surprising. She is just a maid after all."

I sighed. George could be sweet and clever, but his attitude toward servants was somewhere between complete disregard and condescending. Equality of the classes was not a notion that had occurred to his level of society, which made it all the more amazing that Jacob didn't share his manner.

"I wonder where Mrs. White went," I said.

"I wonder *why* she went." We discussed possibilities but without any further information, they were only ideas.

When we reached Druids Way, Jacob reappeared. "There was nothing in Hollowbrooke's office about Mrs. White," he said.

"You didn't rifle through his papers while he was there, I hope." I giggled despite the seriousness of our situation. The picture of Mr. Hollowbrooke's bland face coming alive with horror as his papers rustled was quite amusing.

The corner of Jacob's mouth flicked up in a half-smile. "No. He was elsewhere."

"So Mrs. White left no forwarding address," I said, mostly for George's benefit, "and she lied about her reason for leaving."

We arrived at my house and George sighed. "I think we have officially hit a dead end."

I winced, but he didn't seem to notice his inappropriate choice of words. Not that Jacob seemed to notice either. He stared at me with the familiar intensity that turned my insides to water.

"Your involvement ends here, Emily," he said. "Now."

The footman opened the door so I couldn't tell Jacob he was wrong.

***

I found Celia and Lucy in the kitchen shelling peas. Or rather, Lucy was shelling peas at the central table while my sister sat opposite, the household ledger open in front of her.

"There you are!" Celia said. "Lucy told me you went out with Mr. Culvert. How is he?"

"The same," I said.

"Did you see Mr. Hyde again?"

Of all the questions to ask me, that wasn't the one I expected. "No." I stretched my fingers in front of the warm stove and peered into the pot bubbling away on the hot plate. It looked like the beginnings of broth and smelled delicious. My stomach growled, reminding me I hadn't eaten since breakfast.

I turned around to warm my back and Lucy gave me a smile, something she wouldn't have done a week ago when she first came to work for us. Her wariness of me was definitely lessening. "He seemed very nice, that Mr. Hyde," she said. "Handsome too."

"Very nice," Celia agreed. I had no doubts that if it were in my sister's power, she'd have me betrothed to him within the month.

"Is there anything to eat?" I stole a pea from Lucy's bowl and popped it in my mouth. "I'm hungry." I went to take another pea but Celia smacked my hand away.

"Luncheon was an hour ago." She shut the ledger and blinked innocently up at me, but I wasn't deceived. "Didn't

Mrs. Culvert provide something while you...*researched*?"

I knew that tone. She didn't think I'd been reading books in George's library for a moment. Sometimes I forgot how shrewd Celia could be.

"We weren't researching today. We were visiting an associate of George's to ask him about possession, and about...other things." I didn't want her to know of the possible connection to Blunt and the shape-shifting demon incident. That event had shaken her considerably. Drawing a line between the possession and the demon would certainly give her cause to end my involvement, or at least try to. I could do without the added pressure.

I walked through to the adjoining larder and found some cheese under a cloth and half a loaf of bread. I sliced myself a chunk of each and returned to the kitchen, not bothering with a plate.

Celia clicked her tongue. "Do try to be civil, Em. We are not savages."

I couldn't answer her because my mouth was full, but I sat and leaned over the table to keep her happy. When I'd finished my late lunch, she said, "So you haven't caught the spirit possessing Mr. Arbuthnot yet?"

I swept my hand across the table in an arc, collecting crumbs. "No, but Jacob is going to look for him tonight. If he finds him, we'll try to expel the spirit."

She picked up the ledger and folded it against her chest. "It would seem we have the afternoon free." It was true, we had no séances planned. "Put your coat back on," she said. "We're going out."

***

The omnibus dropped us at Holborn not far from where I'd been earlier at the North London School for Domestic Service. On the whole, Holborn wasn't as destitute as the neighboring Clerkenwell, but it did have pockets of slums huddled in dreary corners, tucked out of sight. I caught glimpses of them down crooked lanes and through crumbling archways as we headed for the Leather Lane market. We were looking for Fran-Swars Something-Foreign.

Where George, Jacob, and I had given up finding Louis' father after Mr. Graves said he couldn't help us, Celia had persisted. While I'd been visiting Price and the School, she'd taken it upon herself to ask other shopkeepers if they remembered the old greengrocer. A butcher recalled he'd opened a stall at the Leather Lane market after leaving Chelsea.

The shops on both sides of Leather Lane were almost invisible behind the carts and stalls that stretched as far as I could see. Shopkeepers shouted promises of the "freshest," the "best," or the "latest fashion from Paris." I stopped to inspect a pair of pale green gloves with beads resembling seed pearls sewn around the edge but Celia dragged me wordlessly away. Not before I realized they weren't silk, despite what the stall-holder said.

My sister had that pinched look to her nose and mouth as if she wished she were anywhere else but Leather Lane. I, on the other hand, had never felt more alive. The street was a narrow pulsing vein threading through the heart of London. The hum of noise ebbed and flowed around me, and the very air throbbed with life. Seeing so many enterprising individuals made me truly believe I was in the world's most energetic city.

Even so, I clutched my reticule tightly. I didn't want to lose what little money I had to a pickpocket, not when there was a pair of pale green gloves to be had for a bargain back at the glover's stall. Silk or not, they were certainly pretty.

With our arms hooked together at the elbows, we strolled side by side in search of François Moreau, greengrocer. Celia had been given his full name by the helpful Chelsea butcher. We asked the first greengrocer we came to and were directed further along. "Next to the lamp man," he said. "Can't miss it."

He was right. The lamp man was visible well before we reached his stall. Strung high up between two vertical poles attached to either end of his cart was a length of rope.

Dozens of hooks were suspended from it like crooked fingers, each one holding a lamp. They swung gently in what little breeze managed to find its way into Leather Lane.

Beside the lamp stall was a small cart with a faded red awning stretching over lettuces, onion, cabbage, and spring fruits. Behind the cart stood a man with tufts of wiry gray hair clinging to his bald head above his ears and sprouting out of his bushy eyebrows like weeds. Deep grooves cut across his forehead and fanned out from the corners of his eyes. He was old but not ancient, a little bent but still tall and strongly built across the shoulders. His skin was darker than mine.

"Mr. Moreau?" Celia asked.

He finished serving his customer before looking at us. I felt Celia stiffen. It must be Louis' father. I could tell she recognized him.

He squinted at her then at me, and the grooves deepened. Then he laughed loudly. He rocked back on his heels and those big shoulders shook. "You!" He kept laughing and it wasn't a friendly laugh. It was a crazy one. The old man—my grandfather—was mad.

"Mr. Moreau," Celia said in a steely voice she occasionally used on me when I'd done something to annoy her. "Mr. Moreau, be quiet, and listen to me."

He stopped laughing at least. "That his girl? My boy's little girl all grown up? He's not here, my boy," he said without waiting for her answer. He spoke with a slight French accent. "He's gone. New South Wales. Long, long gone." There was no hint of wistfulness, no sadness for the son who'd left him. If Mr. Moreau had ever cared for Louis, it was in the past, buried alongside his sanity.

"We're not looking for Louis," Celia said. "We want to see his daughter."

Mr. Moreau pointed at me and started laughing again.

Celia's arm tightened, almost cutting mine in half at the elbow. "I mean his other daughter. She's about ten years old."

"Ah, now. She." He wiped his eyes with the back of his gloveless hand. Little barks of laughter erupted from him as if he couldn't contain them. "She belongs to me, not Louis. Not Louis' girl at all." He lost the fight to control himself and burst into raucous laughter again. A customer who'd been inspecting a lettuce eyed him carefully then backed away. "Your aunt," he said, pointing at me again and grinning like he'd heard the funniest joke. "Cara is Louis' sister, your aunt."

Celia's arm loosened around mine and I heard her draw in a huge, gasping breath as if it was the first she'd taken since arriving in Leather Lane. "Sister?" she said weakly. "So...Louis never came back to London?"

Mr. Moreau shook his head, still grinning. "New South Wales."

Aunt. I had an aunt. And she was younger than me. I would have to think about that later, but for now, there were questions that needed answering. "Are there any other girl children? Yours or Louis'?"

He shrugged and finally stopped laughing. "Maybe. Maybe Louis got another bastard in New South Wales." He suddenly reached across his fruit and vegetables and gripped my chin. His fingers were long, strong. He turned my face to right and left before Celia smacked his arm and he let go. "Huh," was all he said.

"Where can we find Cara?" I asked, rubbing my jaw. His grip hadn't been gentle.

He shrugged again and began to rearrange the onions to fill a gap left from the last sale. "Here. There."

"Where does she live?" Celia said.

"With me."

"Which is where?" I could hear my sister's patience thinning with each word. Another vague answer and it might snap altogether.

His busy fingers stilled. "Why you want to know? She's just a girl." I thought he was being protective of his young daughter until he added, "Not important. Just a girl."

Celia huffed. I gritted my teeth lest I start arguing with the crazy old fool.

"Where can we find her?" Celia persisted. "Tell us, Mr. Moreau. We'll give you money."

I didn't see his reaction because something had caught my attention. Or rather, someone. A small figure. A dark-haired girl. I craned my neck to see around the people and stalls. I let go of Celia and headed up Leather Lane. She called my name. I beckoned for her to follow.

Then I saw her again. The girl. My Aunt Cara.

I ran.

Cara looked up and saw me. She ran off in the opposite direction, weaving between carts and people like it was something she did all the time. I couldn't keep up and lost her at a particularly busy intersection. She could have gone anywhere. I silently cursed.

Celia came up behind me, puffing. "Was that her?" she asked between breaths.

I nodded. "She's gone, but at least we know she lives near here. We could ask around or try Mr. Moreau again."

She made a face. "Talking to that man any more will turn me as crazy as he is." She glanced over her shoulder at Mr. Moreau's stall further down Leather Lane. He was serving a customer and didn't look our way. We were already forgotten.

She sighed. She looked sadder than I'd seen her in a long time, as if buried memories had been dug up and laid bare.

"Do you miss Mama?" I asked gently.

She nodded but kept her gaze on Mr. Moreau. "Every day."

***

I was woken early in the morning by Jacob shaking my shoulder. As soon as my sleepy brain realized it was him, I sat up, alert. If he was visiting me in my bedroom while I was still asleep, it must be important. Ever since we'd sent the demon back, he'd avoided intimacy.

"What is it?" I asked. "What's wrong?"

Morning light edged the drawn curtains and I could see Jacob quite clearly. He moved to the foot of my bed, as far away from me as possible, and stared at me like a startled cat. I expected him to disappear but he didn't. He must have needed to speak to me.

I sat on my bed dressed only in my nightgown, the bedcovers pooled around my hips. His gaze roamed over me, hot and hungry. He licked parted lips. Perhaps he didn't need to speak to me. Perhaps he just needed to see me.

"Everything's wrong," he whispered. "Emily." My name was a breath on his lips, a kiss of air.

I climbed out of bed and went to him. My stockinged feet made no sound on the carpet. It felt like a piece of string was tied to my waist and I was being pulled to him. I couldn't resist, couldn't deviate.

My body slammed into his, my breasts crushed against his rib cage. He groaned and squeezed his eyes shut.

Then he opened them and pushed me away. Hard. I stumbled backward onto the bed.

"Stop," he growled. "No more. We agreed I needed to move on and you should live your life. But I can't if... And you can't..." He shook his head, groaned.

My breath came in short, shallow gasps. My chest felt tight. "I know that's what we decided but...but for now we could have each other. Be together. Just for now."

"No!"

"Jacob?" It came out a whisper, strangled by the unshed tears clogging my throat. "Why—"

"I'm not interested." He strode to the door. "I've been trying to spare you this, but...you forced me to say it."

I felt my heart cave in. It crumbled like an eroded cliff and the pieces tumbled into the gaping hole left behind. It hurt. God, it hurt. "Wh...what do you mean? You told me you loved me." I sounded weak and pathetic. Part of me hated that and was annoyed, but part of me didn't care.

"A week is a long time up there." He jerked his head at the ceiling. "Things change. I've changed."

"Changed?" I shook my head. "Changed how?" How could he stop these feelings? I couldn't, not in a thousand years.

He looked at me. Really looked at me. His eyes were cold and I shivered, suddenly chilled. "I'm dead, Emily. I'm ready to move on. I need to."

I shook my head again. I didn't understand. Need? Ready? I *needed* him, I was *ready* for him. We could take our relationship further. He was a ghost. There would be no consequences like pregnancy. I stretched out my arms, but he put both hands up, halting me.

"Don't," he said in that dead, cold way. "Don't do this to yourself."

"I'm not, *you* are." But his words had served to snap me awake. I felt like I'd been dreaming, but it was no nightmare. It was real. Anger joined the hurt and confusion and eventually won. It was easier that way, safer. I could cope with anger better than sadness.

I had come to terms with Jacob leaving. I had. I wanted him to find peace in the Otherworld where he could wait for me. But my desire for him could not be switched off so easily.

I thought he wanted me just as much.

I was wrong.

"What do you want, Jacob? Why are you here?" I picked up my shawl from where it lay on the stool at my dressing table and wrapped it around my shoulders. I clasped it tightly over my breasts.

Jacob's gaze never shifted from my face. It was still cold and dark. "I found Arbuthnot."

I gasped. "Is he...?"

He shook his head. "He's not dead, but someone else is. He killed a man and the police arrested him. He's in prison."

CHAPTER 8

After breakfast, I told Celia I was going to George's house. It wasn't a lie. I *did* go to George's, and then we traveled by coach to pick up Theo. From there we went to the Leman Street police station in Whitechapel. I gave both George and Theo the details Jacob had given me.

Jacob. He wasn't in the coach with us, thank goodness. I couldn't sit so close to him and not scowl at him or kiss him or...something! I don't know what I wanted to *do*, let alone what I wanted from him.

At least I had a task to occupy my mind. Thinking about Mortlock was infinitely better than thinking about Jacob's rejection.

So I told Theo and George everything that Jacob had told me. Knowing Mortlock and Finch had been acquaintances, Jacob had haunted the East End pubs, brothels, and cock fighting pits near where Finch had lived. Eventually he'd found Mortlock, still occupying Arbuthnot's body. Jacob's plan was to follow him until morning then come and tell me where to find him.

When morning came around, so did the police. They arrested Arbuthnot at dawn in The Bear Ring, a filthy pub in Whitechapel so Jacob said. It took four men to drag him outside while the remaining drunken patrons looked on. When one of his companions asked what he'd done, the officer in charge said, "Murder."

Jacob followed them and learned that a witness had seen Arbuthnot leave the scene of the murder with blood on his hands and clothes. The blood had still been there when the police arrested him.

"A witness," George said. "That's not good."

"Men have been convicted on much less evidence," Theo said. Of the three of us, he looked the most worried. His face was pale and dark circles shadowed his eyes. As Wallace Arbuthnot's cousin, he had every right to be concerned.

"Does Jacob think he did it?" George asked me.

I nodded. "The victim was a well-known troublemaker himself apparently, so it's likely he knew Mortlock. They might have been in the same gang and had a falling out."

"Like Finch," George muttered.

"And the boys he killed before his own death," Theo said. He scrubbed both hands over his face and groaned. "We have to get Wallace out of this mess."

"How?"

"We need a good barrister."

"I have a better idea," I said. "Jacob? Jacob, are you there?"

He appeared and immediately squashed himself into the corner away from me. "What's wrong?"

"We need your help. Do you know the name of the witness who saw Arbuthnot leave?"

He crossed his arms. "Yes."

"Care to share it with us?"

"No."

I clicked my tongue. "Why are you being so...so obstinate?"

"Because I know what you want to do and I don't want you going to visit him."

"Ah. He lives in Whitechapel then."

"You are not going into Whitechapel."

"Excellent," George said, oblivious to Jacob's dark mood. "We were already heading to the Leman Street station. Is it far from there, Beaufort?"

"Does he really think I'm going to allow you to go into Whitechapel?" Jacob asked. But he wasn't looking at George or me. He was watching Theo. His eyes narrowed. His frown deepened.

Sometimes you have to say something you don't want to say, in front of people who don't need to hear your private business. This was one of those times. "I think that after our last conversation, you have no right to tell me where I can and can't go."

George and Theo politely turned their heads to look out the window.

"George, ask the driver to stop," I said. "We'll wait until Jacob tells me where to find the witness."

He did and the coach slowed, coming to a halt at the side of the street. It wasn't busy and there was enough room for other coaches to pass. We could wait there all day if necessary.

Jacob said nothing, so we all sat there. Waiting. The horses whinnied and the coach rocked. Someone outside coughed. Jacob tapped his thigh with his finger like he was playing the same note on a piano over and over. The tapping became faster. The silence grew heavier.

He cracked first. "You're so stubborn, Emily Chambers."

I tried not to smile at my small victory. "Giving me the witness's name and address is the only way," I said. "I have to be involved."

He grunted. "What do you plan on doing to him when you meet him? Force him to retract his statement by beating him with your reticule?"

I thought it rude that he was completely ignoring my companions in his scenario. George probably wouldn't be much help if we needed to use physical force, but Theo looked quite capable. He was tall with broad shoulders and a lean frame. He could turn out to be as useless as George, but

I didn't think so. They bred strong men in the country.

"Yes," I said, miffed. "The reticule will have to do since I didn't bring my parasol."

Jacob gave a snort of laughter that wasn't really a laugh at all.

"Your reticule?" George said. "No need for that, Emily. I have money. How about you, Theo?"

"I don't need money," I said. "I'm not going to buy anything."

"On the contrary. You are going to buy his silence."

"What an excellent idea!" I forked a brow at Jacob. He ignored me and watched as Theo and George checked the wallets tucked into their waistcoat pockets. Between them they had two pounds and ten shillings.

"The address if you please, Jacob," I said.

Grudgingly, he gave it. "But I will be watching the entire time."

"Good. Because if the money doesn't work, we may need to scare him."

***

Jack Rose lived with his wife and five children in a few small rooms in a shabby lodging house in the best part of Whitechapel. "Best" simply meant none of the wretched souls who watched us openly tried to pick our pockets. I suspected a nighttime visit would have a different result.

We'd decided to leave the coach near the police station where it should be safe, and walk from there to Rose's address. That way no one could identify the coach if the police ever questioned Rose's neighbors about his retracted statement. It had been Theo's suggestion and I thought him overstating the competency of our law enforcers by suggesting they would follow up on Rose. But then Jacob said he wanted me to drive all the way in the coach, for safety reasons, and I decided a walk through Whitechapel would be an education if nothing else. I was in a contrary mood where Jacob was concerned. Childish perhaps, but there you have it.

When we first offered the money to Mr. Rose with our instructions for retracting his account, he simply stared at the coins in George's palm. Then he rubbed his chin, pursed his lips and rubbed his chin some more. "I dunno," he said. "Wouldn't be the right thing—"

Mrs. Rose snatched the money out of George's hand before her husband finished. "Tell 'em whatever they want, you stupid fool." With five young children playing on the packed earth floor dressed in nothing but bits of rags sewn together, I didn't blame her for taking it. I only wished we'd had more to give.

"You'll go to the station now," Theo told Rose. "Right away. We'll walk back slowly to allow you time to get there ahead of us."

"No stopping at the pub on the way," George added. He lifted his chin and stared through his spectacles and down his nose at Rose.

Rose was too busy watching his wife stuff the money down the front of her dress to notice his condescending tone.

"That also buys your silence about our visit," Theo said. "Understand? No one is to know we were here."

Mrs. Rose slapped her husband's shoulder. "Did you 'ear the gen'leman?"

"Silence," Rose repeated. "Won't say a word." He grinned, revealing a gap in the middle of his top row of teeth.

"Thank you," I said. "And don't worry, your conscience is clear. We are absolutely certain Mr. Arbuthnot didn't cause that man's death. We just couldn't see any other way to convince the police."

"But I saw him walkin' away."

"No, you didn't." His wife slapped his arm again. "Fool."

***

We arrived at the Leman Street police station after a slow walk through light rain. Theo and George kept pace either side of me like two guards, albeit chatty ones. Jacob walked behind, silent.

The police station was located next to the Garrick Theater. It must be a busy place before and after a penny gaff performance, but it was reasonably quiet when we arrived. George's coach, driver, and footmen waited patiently out front, a collection of excited children once again patting the horses.

Like the rest of Whitechapel, Leman Street was a miserable place. The roads were greasy from the rain, the steps leading up to the front door of the police station in need of repair. Inside, pasted on every wall, police handbills shouted REWARD in bold lettering above smaller writing describing the wanted criminal. A uniformed officer sat at a desk, writing.

"Yes?" he said.

"My cousin is being held here," Theo said. "Mr. Wallace Arbuthnot. Can we see him?"

The officer pointed his quill pen at another uniformed man sitting behind a partition in a kind of office. The upper part of the partition was glass with a square hole cut out so he could talk to us through it. He stood and introduced himself as Inspector Arnold. He wasn't a tall man but was square and bulky like a brick. The collar of his uniform looked tight around his muscular neck and his fat nose was slightly crooked, as if it had been knocked off-center. His black, deep-set eyes raked over us, twice.

We introduced ourselves. Jacob disappeared then reappeared on the other side of the partition. He read the ledger sitting open on the counter top.

Theo repeated his question. Inspector Arnold hesitated then pointed at the ledger. "I was just considering his situation."

"Oh?" Theo was all politeness and innocence. "We understood he'd been arrested for a rather heinous crime. One I can assure you my cousin is not capable of committing."

"He's very upright and gentle-natured," I added.

Inspector Arnold's lips drew together. He regarded me levelly, without condescension for my age or gender. I liked that. "It took four of my men to arrest Mr. Arbuthnot," he said. "Two of them got black eyes for their troubles, one's got sore ribs. My ears are still ringing with language I wouldn't repeat here in front of a lady." He snorted. "Gentle, my ar...foot." He coughed and pretended he wasn't about to say "arse."

"And yet you said you were wondering what to do with him," Theo said. "Does that mean you don't think he did it?"

We waited, watching, holding our breaths. Even Jacob focused on the inspector as if willing him to give in and release Wallace. The longer Inspector Arnold took to answer, the more concerned I became that he didn't believe Jack Rose. That's if Rose had indeed gone straight to the station like we'd asked him to. I wished we'd followed him closer to make sure.

"The witness was just here," Inspector Arnold said, putting me at ease. "Told me he made a mistake and saw nothing. Says he was blind drunk and couldn't have witnessed no one coming nor going from the murder scene."

"There you have it," George said on a breath. "Release Arbuthnot. He's innocent."

Inspector Arnold turned his shrewd gaze on George. George's Adam's apple bobbed furiously. "Not so fast," Arnold said. "He had blood on his hands."

Silence. I could almost hear Theo and George thinking fast, wondering how to explain the blood.

"How did Mr. Arbuthnot say it got there?" I asked.

"He says he doesn't remember."

"It doesn't matter," George said. He tugged on his cuffs and lifted his chin, switching to his gentleman-in-charge persona. "He can't stay in here another minute. People like Wallace Arbuthnot do not commit such terrible crimes. You have the wrong man."

The inspector came out from behind the partition and stood close to George. Very close. He was shorter by a few inches but much wider. He had the sort of arms that could rip tree stumps out of the ground or squeeze the air out of a low-life's chest. George's swallow was audible.

"If you don't keep Culvert quiet," Jacob said, "he's going to ruin any chance you had of getting Arbuthnot released today."

I laid a hand on George's arm. "I can tell you how Mr. Arbuthnot got that blood on his hands, Inspector." The three live men looked at me. "He cut me accidentally last night, you see. There was quite a lot of blood. He mustn't have washed it off."

I could see George and Theo straining not to ask more questions lest it interfere with my story. Jacob knew what cut I was talking about, of course. "Did you have to bring that up here and now?" he said on a sigh. "You know he'll need to see it."

"I don't see no cuts on you, miss," the inspector said.

"It's on my thigh."

George gave a strangled gargle. Theo and the inspector reddened.

"Shall we step behind the partition so I can show you?"

The inspector stretched his neck as if the collar was tightening. He nodded quickly and a shaky hand directed me to go first. It was as if *I* were intimidating *him*, not the other way round.

"I do protest, Emily," George said, frowning.

"It's all right." I moved around to the other side of the partition and the inspector followed. I twirled my finger at George, Theo, and the other policeman at the desk. They dutifully turned their backs. Jacob remained near the counter, his arms crossed and eyes hooded. He didn't look away.

I lifted my skirt and petticoat and unwrapped the bandage above the garter. The cut had begun healing but was still red and puckered. Jacob stood beside the inspector who bent over to inspect the wound.

"He's too close," Jacob said. "Tell him to back away."

Arnold straightened. "Well, Miss..."

"Miss Chambers," I reminded him.

"Well, Miss Chambers, if you can vouch that the blood on Mr. Arbuthnot's hands is your blood and that the cut was done accidentally, I suppose I must release him."

I felt my entire body sigh with relief. "I can."

He nodded and reached out to remove a heavy key hanging from a hook on the wall. "Wait here."

A few minutes later he returned with Wallace Arbuthnot. My first instinct was to clutch Wallace's hand and give it a reassuring squeeze, but then I remembered it wasn't him in there, but Mortlock. He blinked at us in recognition.

"Cousin," Theo said, nodding once. "Your mother will be pleased to have you home."

Mortlock's lip curled. He glanced at the door and rubbed his palms down his stained trousers.

"He's going to run," Jacob said. He disappeared and reappeared at the door.

"You look tired, Mr. Arbuthnot," I said quickly. "Perhaps George and Theo can assist you to the coach."

Both men understood my meaning and grabbed Wallace's arms. He gave a harsh laugh but didn't struggle. Mortlock knew his only way out of jail was to go along with us.

Theo and George marched him out of the police station and into the waiting coach. Jacob and I followed but he held me back before I climbed in.

"There's no room for me," he said. "Call immediately if Mortlock so much as breathes on you. Do you remember the words to send him back?"

I nodded.

"Good. Do it straight away." And then he was gone.

A footman assisted me into the coach and I sat beside George. Theo still held onto his cousin's arm, but Wallace's eyes were closed, his body slumped so that his knees touched mine. He looked to be asleep. Perhaps he was still drunk.

"*Return, Spirit, to your rightful place,*" I chanted.

Wallace stirred, making obscene snuffling noises through his nose.

I focused on the words of the incantation. "*Return to the—*"

His eyes suddenly opened, and I jumped in alarm. "Miss Chambers?" He sounded different, normal, like Wallace Arbuthnot should sound.

I leaned forward. "Mr. Arbuthnot? How do you feel?"

He sat up and rubbed his eyes. "My head hurts like the devil."

That's because the devil had been inside it. I glanced at Theo. He smiled, sheer relief imprinted in every feature. I smiled back. Mortlock was gone.

"Wallace?" Theo said. "Are you well, Cousin?"

Wallace cupped his hands over his mouth and drew in a deep breath. He coughed. "Good lord." He screwed up his nose and drew his hands away. "Is that...blood?" His soft face paled.

"It's all right," I said gently. "Do you remember anything of the past day or two?"

He shook his head and looked down at his clothes. "Bloody hell! Look at the state of me! Where have I been?" He turned to his cousin. "Theo?"

"Painting," Theo said quickly. "Isn't that right, Mr. Culvert?"

"Culvert?" Wallace echoed. He frowned at George. George nodded once. "Miss Chambers, what are you doing here? And why have I been painting? I don't remember anything."

"You've been ill," I said. "You need rest. You've been wandering around the city and we've been looking for you. But you're better now and we'll take you home. It's likely you won't ever recall anything of the past two days."

He nodded dully. "Right. Painting." He stared at his hands and I suspected he didn't believe us but was too afraid to probe further lest he discover an unpalatable truth. "How extraordinary."

Beside me, George grunted. He removed his glasses, put them on again, removed them once more then returned them to his face. He looked at Theo and Wallace and laughed.

"Something funny, George?" I asked.

He said nothing and turned his shoulder to me and stared out the window. Wallace closed his eyes and appeared to fall asleep.

Theo watched me. It was disconcerting at first. I tried not to touch my hair to see if it was out of place. Then he smiled and I couldn't help but return it.

The coach pulled to a stop at the Arbuthnots' Kensington residence and Wallace woke up with a snort and splutter. For a brief moment I thought Mortlock had returned, but then he seemed to remember where he was and the gentlemanly manner returned.

"Goodbye, Miss Chambers." He gave me a self-conscious smile and ran his hands over his wayward tufts of hair. No doubt he felt strange without a hat.

"Will you visit us tomorrow?" Theo asked me. "To discuss the Jacob Beaufort matter, as you originally planned," he added.

"If your cousin is feeling better," I said. Tomorrow would be good. The sooner we could pick up the trail to Jacob's killer, the better. He needed to move on. I might not want him to and I might not like the thought of him leaving me, but I could sense it whenever he was near. For whatever reason, he needed to leave this realm.

Theo clasped my hand and kissed it. "Until then. Emily." He kissed it again then climbed out of the coach after his cousin.

George banged the roof and the coach rolled forward. "Home!" he shouted.

I stared at my hand where Theo had kissed it. I didn't know what to think. He was sweet and kind, the perfect gentleman. I liked him. But that was all. Just like. It wasn't the same as how I felt about Jacob. I sighed and closed my eyes. I felt so tired. All I wanted to do was return home and find something to eat then while away the rest of the day in the parlor with my sister. Beside me, I could feel George shift on the seat.

"Why do you think Mortlock didn't transfer into one of the policemen when he had the chance?" I asked George. "He could have been free then."

George chuckled, a low sound coming from the depths of his throat. "Too drunk. That fat sod couldn't handle his ale. Useless slab of lard."

I opened my eyes and frowned at him. And then my heart tripped over itself. *No. Dear God, no.*

George pushed his glasses up his nose and turned to face me. His lips twisted into a grin that held no humor, no friendship. All evil.

I screamed.

He lunged.

CHAPTER 9

George, or rather Mortlock, leaned over me, his knees on the seat straddling my thighs. Close. So disgustingly close. I tried to wriggle away, beat him off, but he pinned my shoulders against the seatback and I couldn't move my arms, not with any effectiveness.

He licked my neck. I gagged and twisted my head from side to side. If he kissed me on the mouth, I might throw up.

He pressed himself against me, smothering my face in his jacket.

Air. I needed air. Couldn't breathe. I had to get away, get him off. I felt dizzy. My chest hurt. My throat closed up.

Fighting panic, I did the only thing I could think of—I jerked my knee up into his groin.

He sucked in air between this teeth and let it out in a small, high-pitched whine. He didn't let go but his body slackened just enough for me to use my arms again. I shoved his chest as hard as I could and he stumbled backwards onto the opposite seat.

He clutched his chest and grunted.

I thought fast. I could call Jacob, but there was nothing he could do. There were no weapons in the cabin and his fists were useless against George. I could shout at the driver and footmen, but they probably wouldn't pummel their master no matter what I said. So I did the only thing in my power to do.

I chanted the incantation to return Mortlock. "*Return, Spirit, to your rightful place.*"

His eyes widened. "Stop!"

"*Return to the Otherworld where you belong. Return—*"

"Shut it!" He half-stood, hunched beneath the low roof.

And then he hit me.

Burning pain spread like fire across my jaw and cheek. I toppled into the corner and tucked my legs up, making myself as small as possible, bracing myself for the next blow.

It didn't come. He opened the door and jumped out of the moving coach. The door banged shut behind him. I gasped and scrambled to the window to see if he was injured, only to be thrown back when the driver pulled hard on the reins.

"Whoa," he said to the horses.

The coach rocked as the footmen jumped down. I heard them call after George, questioning but polite. A moment later, one of them opened the door.

"Miss Chambers?" He hesitated but his curiosity must have got the better of him. "Why did Mr. Culvert leave in such a hurry?"

I covered my jaw with my hand. I couldn't feel the soft kid leather of my glove through the riot of pain. "He...was in a hurry." Pathetic, but I could think of no clever explanation. My mind had gone numb. "Take me home, please."

"Very well, miss." He picked my bonnet up off the floor where it must have fallen when Mortlock hit me and held it out. I took it and placed it on the seat beside me. He shut the door. If he didn't believe my explanation, he didn't show it.

I closed my eyes and blew out a breath. Jacob would have to be told. He would have to repeat his searches all over again, this time for George. I wanted to wait until I got home and checked the damage to my face in a mirror, but that would waste valuable time. He needed to know now so he could start immediately.

Well, this would be an interesting little interlude. Not that I could be completely sure of Jacob's reaction to anything involving me lately. The messages I received from him were decidedly mixed.

I tried various ways of covering my jaw with my hand and settled on a thoughtful pose with one arm crossed over my stomach and the other elbow resting on it. With my fingers lightly touching my cheek, I think I looked nonchalant, relaxed. I felt anything but.

"Jacob? Jacob, can you come, please?"

He appeared on the seat opposite just as the coach moved forward. "Why are you alone?"

"Theo and Wallace have returned to the Arbuthnot residence, and George has...left." I paused. There was no easy way to say it. "Mortlock is now possessing him."

If he was capable of going white, he would have at that moment. He groaned and rubbed his hands through his hair and dragged them down his face. "You'd better tell me everything."

I did. Almost. I told him how we thought Mortlock had returned to the Waiting Area of his own volition but had soon discovered he was inside George.

"Wait," he said. "I'm confused about the timing. Did you notice the switch straight away, while Theo and Wallace were still here?" He held his hands out, palms up, questioning. "If so, why didn't you call me immediately instead of waiting until after you took them home? And at what point did Mortlock jump out of the coach?"

"Er..."

His eyes narrowed and he gave me that familiar piercing gaze that made it feel like he could read my mind. Getting answers that way might have been quicker than waiting for me to give them. I didn't know what to say and his increasingly dark glare put me on edge.

"I, uh, well, we were sitting here, talking. Um, no that's not right. I think..."

"Emily." His soft voice, so at odds to his fierce demeanor, silenced me. It didn't stop my body from shaking.

Why was I shaking? And crying?

Tears slipped down my cheeks, seeped under my fingers, and stung the sore skin at my jaw. I couldn't stop them.

Suddenly he was sitting beside me, having switched places with my bonnet. He circled his arms around my shoulders and gently pulled me to his chest. Our thighs touched. My head tucked neatly under his chin and my nose pressed into his throat. He had no smell, no pulse, no warmth, but I felt instantly better. Safer. I curled my fingers into his cool shirt. My other hand still hovered over my jaw.

Not for long. Oh-so tenderly, he drew it away. "No." His voice was a thready whisper. "No, no, no, no." He cradled the side of my face. His fingers reached into the hair curling behind my ear and his thumb traced the outline of what I assumed was a darkening bruise. I didn't dare look at him, didn't dare breathe lest he stop touching me. It felt too good, soothing, like cool water on a burn. I ached for his touch, but it seemed wrong that it had taken a horrible incident to bring us together.

We stayed like that until the coach pulled to a stop outside my house. The footman opened the coach door and helped me down the step to the pavement. Jacob was already on my front porch, looking very much as he had the first day I met him—arms and ankles crossed in a lazy stance, one shoulder leaning against the door frame. A glance at his face gave a very different story. Whatever tenderness he'd felt as he held me had been wiped away.

I waited until the coach left before I spoke. "Aren't you going to look for George?"

"Soon."

"What are you waiting for?"

"For you to get inside."

Ah. My safety first. "Jacob..."

"Don't. Emily..." He half-sighed and half-groaned and lowered his arms. "I'm sorry I wasn't there for you. I...I'm having trouble being near you." He shook his head, closed his eyes briefly. "It won't happen again. I'm not going to let Mortlock hurt you anymore. I promise."

I must have still been out of sorts because I couldn't think of a response. My tongue felt thick and my head hurt. All I wanted to do was curl up with him again, be held by him. I stepped closer and pressed my palm over his dead heart. Tears welled but I forced them away. No more crying.

I might have stopped the tears, but I still couldn't think what to say. My heart overflowed with emotions and turmoil, but the right words escaped me.

The door suddenly opened and Lucy stood there, smiling. "I thought I saw you through the window, miss. Why are you just standing there? Come in. Miss Chambers is in—" She squinted. Gasped. "Oh my! Your face!" She ushered me inside and shut the door.

Jacob hadn't followed.

Lucy was too good a servant to ask me what happened. She silently took my gloves, bonnet, and coat, but her gaze kept flicking to my jaw and she squeezed her lips together as if trying to hold in her questions. If I didn't tell her something soon she might burst.

I peered into the big mirror hanging on the wall and cringed. A blue-black bruise bloomed from my jaw to my cheek. There would be no hiding it from anyone, especially my hawk-eyed sister.

As if I'd summoned her, she came down the stairs. "You're back," she said. "Did you achieve much at Mr. Culvert's library?"

I nodded. "A great deal." I kept the bruised side of my face away from her. Perhaps I could edge past her and slink away to my room—

"Emily, what's wrong?"

So much for slinking. "Nothing!"

She met me at the base of the stairs. "Why are you looking at me sideways?"

Lucy rearranged the flowers in the vase on the table

beneath the mirror, turning it this way and that. She was stalling, wanting to hear the exchange between Celia and myself.

I turned my face so Celia could see the bruise. Like Lucy, she gasped. "Good lord! What happened?"

"I accidentally walked into a door."

Celia gently touched my chin and inspected the bruise. She said nothing for a long time and I felt certain she'd seen through my lie. "Lucy, fetch the Holloway's Ointment."

Lucy hurried away. Celia let go of me. "Is that ghost here?" she asked.

"Jacob? No. Why?"

"Because I have something to say to him."

"What is it?"

She lifted her skirts and stomped back up the stairs. "This is his fault and I want to tell him to fix it."

"Celia!" I raced up the stairs after her. "I walked into a door!"

She paused and fixed me with a glare so full of anger I took a step back down. "Do *not* lie to me."

I gulped. "What happened is not Jacob's fault. It's Mortlock's and whoever summoned him out of the Waiting Area."

She continued on up. "I've entrusted you into his care and that of George Culvert for the duration of this task. Any harm that comes to you is entirely their fault for not protecting you."

"George is the one who did it," I said, giving in. She stopped again. The anger was replaced by real concern. "The spirit of Mortlock is now possessing him," I said. "I almost sent him back but...he stopped me. It's not Jacob's fault, Celia."

She humphed. "I'll cancel this evening's soiree séance at Mrs. Underwood's. You're in no fit state to be seen by clients."

"No, don't cancel. It'll be dark and I'll turn my face away from them." I needed to keep my mind off thoughts of

Mortlock, George, and Jacob. Most of all Jacob, because one question repeated itself over and over.

Why had he been so tender toward me when he claimed to no longer love me?

***

I woke up late the next morning. Jacob wasn't waiting for me in my room or in the parlor where Lucy served breakfast. I thought he might visit to see how I was, or give me an update on George's whereabouts, but he didn't. I tried not to show my disappointment to Celia who sat in an armchair near the window and pretended to be sewing and not watching me.

Neither of us spoke until Lucy returned, a bright smile lighting up her face. "This just arrived, Miss Chambers." Excitement bubbled out of her as she handed Celia a thick cream envelope sealed with red wax. "The address is written in a very elegant hand." She busied herself plumping cushions as Celia opened it.

"It's an invitation," Celia said, reading.

"From whom?" I asked.

She blinked at me, her lips slightly parted. "I do hope that bruise heals quickly."

I took the invitation. It was from Lady Preston, requesting our presence at Adelaide's coming out ball. I stared at Celia. She stared back at me.

Lucy paused in her vigorous plumping and looked ready to have a fit if we didn't tell her. So I told her. She gave a small squeal and almost tore the cushion apart in her enthusiasm. "Oh, Miss Chambers, what shall you wear?"

I didn't know to which of us she spoke, but it didn't matter. Both Celia and I had nothing fit to wear to a ball thrown by Lord and Lady Preston. It would be a grand affair. The most notable people of London would be there, possibly dukes and duchesses, or even princes!

I sat down. Stood up. Sat down again. Lucy grinned at me. "We'll need new gowns made," I said. "Something elegant and pretty. Modern. Shall we go to the dressmakers?

113

Today? I wonder how much it'll cost."

"Too much for the both of us," Celia said on a sigh. "But you, my dear, will have the finest gown of all the young ladies."

My heart sank. "But you must too! Surely we can afford two gowns. Two modest ones."

She shook her head with finality. "There is no point having two modest gowns. You must have one very elegant one." When I shook my head, she put aside her sewing and stood in front of me. She clasped my shoulders and looked me in the eyes. "This is your chance to shine, Emily. You will shine regardless of what you wear, but you will shine brighter if you have the right gown."

"But you—"

"My time has past." There was no bitterness in her tone, no regret, only enthusiasm. Her eyes shone with it. "Yours is just beginning. You can secure your future at this ball."

I jerked out of her grip. Why did it have to be about marriage? Why couldn't I have some fun, enjoy new experiences and meet new people without always evaluating potential husbands?

"I thought you had me married off to George or Theo already."

She ignored me and re-read the invitation again. "Miss Beaufort must consider you a particular friend to have invited you."

I shrugged. The conversation about marriage and ball gowns was left alone. For now. I was sure both would rear their heads again in the near future. "I wonder if Lord Preston knows I am on the guest list," I said.

"Oh, I nearly forgot!" Lucy delved into her apron pocket and produced another letter. She handed it to Celia who opened it and read.

"It's also from Lady Preston," my sister said. "She's invited us both to luncheon."

Either Lord Preston was out, or he'd changed his mind about my presence in his household.

***

Lord Preston was indeed at his club, but Adelaide assured me he would not throw me out when we arrived for the ball in three weeks time. Which didn't mean they had told him I was invited. Perhaps Adelaide and Lady Preston didn't plan on telling him until the final moment when it was too late. That's what I would do.

"I'm so pleased you can come," Adelaide said.

She and I sat apart from Celia and Lady Preston in the large, golden drawing room. We'd finished our light lunch and the footman had served tea to extend our pleasant afternoon. Celia and Lady Preston seemed to be getting along quite well, despite the age difference. I put Adelaide's mother's age in her early forties—although she was so beautiful and slender that I could have been quite wrong— and Celia was thirty-three.

"I must thank you for inviting us," I said. "I'm not sure who's more excited, myself or Celia."

Adelaide giggled. "You have been so good to us and Mother has really taken to you. As have I," she added shyly. "I don't get to see many of my friends lately unless we invite them over. Mother has become very protective, even more so after your warning. She doesn't let me go anywhere."

"Oh. Sorry."

"It's not your fault. I would rather be forewarned of the danger. Do you think this business will all be over by the ball?"

Disappointing or worrying her would just be cruel so I nodded. "I'm sure it will be. Jacob is looking for George now."

"George? Do you mean that nice Mr. Culvert? Why is Jacob looking for him?"

Oh dear, I'd forgotten she knew little of what had happened. I explained to her about Mortlock's spirit and how it was now inside George. I left out the particulars of her own involvement and that of the girl, my Aunt Cara. Whether she knew there was more to the story or not, she gave no indication.

"Poor Mr. Culvert," she said. Her pretty brow furrowed and she took my hand. "We must do something for him before...before..."

I nodded. There was no need to complete the sentence. We both knew what a man like Mortlock was capable of doing and what emotional scars his actions would leave on a gentle soul like George. He would be horrified if his hands committed a mortal sin, even if he had no control over them.

"What *can* we do?" she asked. "What can I do?"

I blew out a breath. "Not a great deal. It's up to Jacob to find him and when he does I'm not sure he'll notify me of his whereabouts this time although I am one of only two people who can send him back." I gingerly touched the bruise on my jaw.

"The spirit did that?" Adelaide must have noticed it earlier, but she hadn't asked how I'd got it. Well-brought-up ladies left such potentially sensitive matters alone. Now that I had drawn attention to it, she would have felt free to ask.

"It did."

She shook her head, slowly, as if trying—and failing—to understand how a man could hit a woman. The men in her world were so genteel, so proper and chivalrous, that men like Mortlock must be a bafflement.

"Jacob will kill him," she suddenly spat. Her eyes turned the same ice-cold blue of her brother's when he was angry. Her venom surprised me. I didn't think she was capable of such hatred.

"Mortlock is already dead," I said, rather stupidly. I knew she'd meant it figuratively and not literally. "The only way to send his spirit back is to have a medium do it. There is one other, but she's the one who summoned him here in the first place. Jacob will come to me when he finds George. He has to." I said it as much to convince myself as Adelaide. Jacob had few options, and I was the most likely of them, but that didn't mean he would come to me. Not after his vow to keep me safe.

***

There was little I could do and I wanted to do *something*. Sitting at home didn't appeal to me, so I decided to visit Wallace and Theo. Hopefully Wallace would be up to answering my questions about a certain Frederick from his Oxford year.

Kensington wasn't far and it was a pleasant enough day for a walk, if a little cool. It didn't take much convincing for Celia to agree to accompany me. With George temporarily occupied, Theo was the next choice on her eligible-men-who-might-wed-Emily list.

Mrs. Arbuthnot greeted us enthusiastically enough, even if she seemed a little bemused by our visit since I didn't give an explanation. However, as I suspected, her desire to gossip overrode any awkwardness she must have felt at entertaining ladies normally outside her social circle. Mentioning that we'd just come from Lady Preston's house certainly helped. It seemed the Arbuthnots had also received invitations to Adelaide's ball.

"And how is the lovely Miss Beaufort?" she asked. The mention of Adelaide's name was clearly an attempt to draw her son's attention to her. Indeed, Wallace sat up straighter and echoed his mother's question.

"Yes, how *is* Miss Beaufort? The last time she was here she seemed a little out of sorts."

Theo and I exchanged glances. He shook his head slightly. It would seem he hadn't told his cousin about the possession of Adelaide and Wallace. Very wise. Wallace did not seem like the sort of person who would take the news well.

"Better," I said. I almost told him that she would enjoy a visit from him and his mother to break up her long days at home but held my tongue. Unleashing Wallace and Mrs. Arbuthnot on Adelaide and Lady Preston might not be something they would welcome. If it were George however—minus the spirit of Mortlock—I suspected the reception would be quite different. The way Adelaide had enthusiastically asked after him was rather telling. George would be pleased.

"And have you recovered from your recent illness, Mr. Arbuthnot?" I asked.

He pushed out his chest which unfortunately also pushed out his stomach. The last time I sat in Mrs. Arbuthnot's drawing room his buttons had popped off. He wore a different waistcoat, but I kept an eye on it nevertheless. "Fit as a fiddle," he said.

"I'm so pleased to hear it." I was about to launch into the reason for our visit when Theo spoke first.

"Are you well, Emily?" He occupied the chair closest to where I sat beside Celia on the sofa and leaned forward slightly. All earnestness.

The bruise. I'd almost forgotten it. "Quite well, thank you. Much better than the door that gave me this, however. It's rather worse for our collision."

Wallace laughed and his entire body wobbled like jelly. Mrs. Arbuthnot and Celia were still discussing the ball and didn't appear to hear. Theo regarded me levelly and rubbed a finger over his lips, thoughtful. I knew he didn't believe me.

"Mr. Arbuthnot," I said before Theo could question me further, "I hoped you could tell me more about Frederick, the one you knew at Oxford."

Wallace shrugged. "Not much to tell, Miss Chambers. He was in my year along with Beaufort. I didn't know him well."

"What are you doing here?" Jacob's voice, coming from behind, startled me.

I half-turned to look at him but stopped and kept my gaze on Wallace. I didn't want to alert anyone to his presence. "What was Frederick's last name? Do you recall?" Hopefully that was enough of an explanation for Jacob.

Jacob sighed and came around to stand at the end of the sofa near me. "This could have waited until after the Mortlock business was finished. I don't like you wandering around the city on your own."

I ignored him and gave my full attention to Wallace. His

mouth twisted to one side in thought, then the other. I glanced at Theo. He stared back at me without smiling. He seemed lost in his own thoughts.

"Ah!" Wallace thumped his hand on the chair arm. "I remember now. Frederick Seymour. Nice enough fellow, came from a good family, long lineage, fallen on hard times I believe. Strange thing about his parents, though. He lived alone with his father, but when I made a reference to his mother's passing, he said she wasn't dead. He never did tell me where she was. Very odd. Don't you agree?"

"Oh yes, very," I echoed. "I wonder if the name Frederick Seymour will mean anything to Lady Preston." It was said for Jacob's benefit, but he didn't seem to hear me. He was too intent on looking at Theo who in turn was looking at me. We made a strange little intense triangle.

"You mentioned during our last visit that Frederick died," I said to Wallace. "Do you know how?"

"Yes. Terrible business. He killed himself."

CHAPTER 10

"Suicide!" Jacob shook his head. "That can't be right."

"Dear lord," Theo said, his focus no longer on me but on his cousin.

"Are you sure he killed himself?" I asked Wallace. "There was no doubt?"

"None whatsoever." Despite the awful subject matter, Wallace seemed rather pleased with himself, enjoying his role as news bearer. "He was seen jumping off a bridge into the upper Thames one evening. A passerby dove in to try and save him, but it had been raining heavily and the current was strong. His body was found the following day downstream. Awful business."

"No." Jacob shook his head. "He's wrong. I killed him. I know I did. My...my killer said so."

It did seem odd. His killer had accused Jacob of causing his son's death. The only possible person he might have killed was Frederick Seymour after they fought one night. Although Frederick had got up and run away, Jacob assumed he'd died hours or days later from a head wound. If Wallace was correct, Jacob hadn't played a part in Frederick's death at all. At least, not directly. There was always the possibility Frederick had killed himself over something Jacob had said or done.

"He was their only child apparently," Wallace said.

"So very sad," I murmured.

"Quite shocking," Theo said. "But does it help you at all, Miss Chambers?"

"Not at all." We were back where we'd started and I for one had no ideas for what to do next. It was very disheartening.

Theo's smile was warm, encouraging. "You're clever. I'm sure you'll work it out."

Jacob grunted. "Emily, you need to make excuses. I know where George is."

Why didn't he say so before! George may have already moved on.

"Celia, is it time to go?" I asked rather bluntly.

She scowled through her polite veneer. "I was discussing something of importance with Mrs. Arbuthnot."

"It's just that I'm feeling a little tired."

Her scowl deepened. She must know I was making excuses to leave. "I do apologize, Mrs. Arbuthnot," Celia said, rising. "Perhaps we can continue this conversation another time."

Mrs. Arbuthnot tried to rock her bulky frame out of the chair, but after three attempts, gave up and simply waved us off from where she sat.

Theo and Wallace walked us out. Whether by design or accident, Wallace and Celia forged ahead leaving Theo and I behind. We weren't alone. Jacob stayed close, his dark mood throwing a shadow over me.

"Emily, *are* you all right?" Theo asked, gently touching my elbow.

"I'm well. Thank you for your concern."

He didn't look convinced. "How did you get that bruise? And I want an honest answer this time."

"Tell him it's none of his business," Jacob said.

"I...uh..."

"The spirit did it, didn't he?" Theo said. "Mortlock? Am I

right in thinking he hasn't left?"

"He's still on this realm." I didn't want to tell him Mortlock had transferred to George. He'd realize he'd left me alone in the coach with him and feel terrible. That wouldn't be fair. None of this was his fault.

Theo's grip tightened on my elbow, reassuring.

"Tell him to let go," Jacob growled. "Now."

I said nothing. I liked Theo's comforting touch and did *not* like Jacob telling me what to do. My lack of response drew raised eyebrows from him. Then a long, slow blink.

Theo stopped me at the top of the curving staircase. Celia and Wallace were already halfway down, deep in conversation. Theo clasped both my hands lightly in his and rubbed his thumbs along my knuckles. It would have been soothing and gentle if Jacob didn't tower over me, hands on hips. For a brief moment I thought he might do something wicked to frighten Theo, but he didn't. He did something most unexpected—he turned his back, giving us privacy.

Even so, he was close enough to hear us and close enough for me to see the rigidity across his shoulders, the tap-tap of his finger on the gleaming polished balustrade.

"If there's anything I can do," Theo said, "I want you to come to me immediately. I want to help in any way I can." He glanced over his shoulder, down the stairs to my sister and his cousin. They weren't watching. His hand skimmed lightly across my bruised jaw. The touch was different to Jacob's, warmer, but no less affectionate.

My heart tripped over itself then swelled to twice its size. Theo was a handsome man and his attention was focused entirely on me. What girl wouldn't like that?

Jacob, standing beside us, half-turned to see me. His finger stopped tapping. He went very still and stared at the place where Theo's hand hovered. It was impossible to know what he was thinking or feeling.

It felt like all the air became denser around us, like it was closing in, suffocating. I couldn't breathe. I stepped away from Theo and his hands dropped to his sides.

"Thank you." I had to get out, had to breathe. I descended the stairs as fast as my skirts would allow and gave cursory goodbyes at the door.

Once outside and my lungs filled with air again, I glanced back. Theo stood inside the doorway, a tentative, confused smile on his lips. Jacob and Wallace were nowhere in sight.

Celia hooked her arm through mine and marched me off down the street. I looked around for Jacob, expecting him to appear and direct me to George, but he didn't. So I walked and my sister chatted.

"Are you listening?" Celia asked after a few moments.

"Yes, of course."

"Then what did I just say?"

"Er, that Mrs. Arbuthnot is a very entertaining woman?"

She clicked her tongue. "I said she seemed nice enough and very eager to talk. Do you know what she talked about?"

"The weather?"

Another click of her tongue. "She talked about you."

"Me?"

"Well, not directly."

"Celia, you're not making sense. How can she talk about me *in*directly?"

We turned the corner. Still no sign of Jacob. Where *was* he? Mortlock could be getting away and then we'd have to hunt him all over again.

"She mentioned that her son was going to marry well," Celia went on. "That was her way of telling me he's not available for you."

I barked out a laugh. "I could have told you that."

"You're not offended?"

"Of course not. I wouldn't take Wallace Arbuthnot as my husband even if he were a prince."

She sniffed. "You most certainly would. But he's not a prince, so this discussion is silly."

I couldn't agree more. Any discussion involving me and marriage was silly.

"Mrs. Arbuthnot also told me her nephew plans to study

law," Celia went on. "She gave no indication as to her thoughts on *his* eligibility to wed you."

"You didn't let her think I was interested in Theo, did you?"

"You do like him, don't you? He's very handsome."

"Ye-es." How could I explain what I felt when I wasn't entirely sure myself? Besides, I wasn't ready for marriage. I wasn't sure if I would ever be. "Law takes a long time to study," I said trying to sound bored. Perhaps if she thought me disinterested, she'd leave the topic alone.

"You could secure a promise from him now and marry when he's finished his studies. Once he enters into practice, he'll need a good wife to set up house for him. *And* he likes you. Mrs. Arbuthnot said he couldn't stop talking about you."

"Really?" My face heated. So much for giving nothing away.

Celia patted my arm, smug. "So you *do* like him."

I sighed. "Never mind." I liked Theo, but was there anything more than that? It was very difficult to see clearly with Jacob around, muddying the waters. My feelings for *him* were so strong, it was hard to imagine ever feeling that way about anyone else. But what if he wasn't here?

Just as I thought it, he appeared beside me. He slipped something hard and cool into my hand and closed my fingers around it so no one, including me, could see it.

"We need to find George," he said. "Can you get away now?"

If I told Celia I was going shopping, she would want to come to make sure I didn't spend too much money. If I told her I was going for a walk, she would also insist on accompanying me. I had to choose something she would consider dull and since I couldn't visit George's library without him home and she knew it, there was only one other option.

"I'm going into the museum this afternoon," I said. "There's an exhibition of prehistoric artifacts. Do you mind?

I'll be home for dinner."

"The museum? Oh Emily, do you *have* to? Gentlemen don't like clever girls."

I unhooked my arm from hers. "Then if any gentlemen come calling this afternoon, don't tell them where I am."

Jacob gave a short snort of either laughter or derision. It was hard to tell which.

Celia gave me a withering look. "Very well, go to the museum. Be sure to be home before dark and if that Beaufort boy wants you to send that awful spirit back..." She sighed and waved a hand. "I suppose you'd better help him." Her gaze wandered around, not really focusing on anything. "But tell him that I will *not* be pleased if any harm comes to you. Not pleased at all." Did she guess that he was nearby?

"Yes, Celia." I pecked her cheek and we parted. I fell into step alongside Jacob. We walked in silence down a narrow, quiet residential street with very similar style houses as the Arbuthnots'—tall, slender and handsome in red and cream. It felt like we were at the bottom of a steep chasm and even though the sun was out, its warmth didn't reach us.

"Your sister has strange notions about what gentlemen do and don't like in a woman," Jacob said after a while.

"That's probably why she's still unwed. Jacob, what do you think of Frederick Seymour's death?"

"One problem at a time. First we send Mortlock back, then we worry about my situation."

That was the end of that. Silence stretched. I tried to think of something to say to break the awkwardness. I didn't like the strangeness surrounding us. I wanted to return to the easy banter we'd shared in the past. And the affection.

"Are you angry with me?" I asked him.

He took a long time to answer. "No. I can't be angry with you."

"Oh. Then...why are you so cold to me lately?"

Another long pause. He stopped and I stopped too. We faced each other. "Emily, I...I just want you to be careful with that fellow."

"Theo? Why?"

He looked down at his feet. "You're not going to like my answer."

"Tell me anyway."

I expected him to say he was jealous. No, I *hoped* he would say he was jealous. Admitting he loved me and wanted me all to himself would be quite a pleasing response. My heart leapt into my throat at the prospect.

"Theo is not a rich man."

My heart returned to its rightful position with a dull thud. "I know that."

He looked up at me through his long lashes, his head still bowed. "Rich gentlemen can wed whomever they want. Poor ones can't."

I blinked at him. "Are you saying he won't make me an offer?"

He winced. "I suppose I am. Whatever he feels for you..." He cleared his throat. "Whatever he feels for you won't matter. He can't marry you and keep the life he enjoys as an idle gentleman."

"But he won't be idle! He's going to be a lawyer! His aunt told Celia so."

He looked at me. Just looked. His blue eyes, usually so bright, dulled to slate gray. "Most gentlemen have been bred into a life of idleness, even country ones. Becoming a lawyer requires a lot of hard work. I don't know Theo well but—"

"Exactly, you don't know him. And have you forgotten that you're a gentleman too?"

"Was," he said. "That's why I know him and his kind."

I had nothing to say to that. Why was everyone discussing marriage—*my* marriage? Why was Jacob?

"You're worse than Celia," I snapped. "And that surprises me."

He sighed. "It surprises me too." He stormed ahead. "You need to catch an omnibus or hire a hansom. It's too far to walk."

It seemed our conversation had ended. I probably should

have been glad, but I wished we'd ended it on *my* terms.

***

The omnibus dropped us in Shoreditch, a neighboring suburb of Mortlock's haunt of Whitechapel. The suburbs shared more than a border, however. Like Whitechapel, "The Ditch" squeezed as many of London's poor into its narrow, crumbling tenements that would fit. Miserable faces peered out of grimy windows and dirty children tugged the hem of my skirt as I passed them playing on the muddy cobbles. Most of the able-bodied men must have been at work because the only ones I saw were either drunk or elderly, their bodies bent from decades of hard labor.

"Stay near me," Jacob said, scanning the street. I couldn't possibly get any closer. Our hips almost touched. Our hands were linked but that was so he could quickly access the knife I gripped. We'd decided I should hold the little weapon he'd found in Wallace's room so as not to draw attention to a floating object. The blade was an ingenious device that folded neatly into the handle and flicked out when a button was pressed.

Being so close to him tore me apart. On the one hand I enjoyed being with him, but on the other, I was still angry. I wanted to tell him Theo wasn't the sort to give up if he really wanted something, but I couldn't be sure if that were true. Or if indeed he wanted me enough.

"Mortlock was dead drunk when I found him," Jacob said. "So he's probably still asleep on his bed."

His bed was in a rented room located on the fifth floor of a long tenement building. Broken lamps arched over the doorways of the shops occupying the ground floor. On the higher floors, dozens of iron balconies stretched from one end to the other like railway tracks. Two of the balconies had flowerpots, but all the flowers were dead, and many had washing flung over railings. I didn't think the linen would be particularly clean after spending the day in the sooty air.

We were about to climb the stairs when a man half-ran and half-stumbled down them. He staggered from side to side and would have bumped into me but Jacob pulled me out of the way just in time. The man lurched out of the stairwell doorway onto the street, his cloak billowing behind him.

"That was him!" Jacob said.

"George?" The man had the same build as George and his chin had the beginnings of a scraggly beard. I hadn't seen the rest of his face so it *could* have been him.

Jacob ran. I followed, clutching the knife tighter, and almost slammed into the shopkeeper coming out of his broker's shop.

"Watch it!" He hefted a box down from a cart parked out the front. I looked past it, left and right, but Jacob and George had disappeared.

"You lookin' for that ghost what went past?"

I spun around. A woman stood there in a nightdress that might have once been white but was now gray and red. The gray was from age and grime. The red was blood. It covered her from waist to knees.

She was dead. If the blood wasn't enough of an indicator, her fuzzy edges gave it away. She looked like a piece of fabric that had been washed too many times.

I glanced up and down the street. There were quite a few people around. Too many for me to want to fall into conversation with a ghost. They already regarded me strangely, as if I didn't belong there. They might run me out of Shoreditch if they saw me talking to myself.

The ghost smiled, revealing a lone tooth on her bottom gum and another on her top. She tossed her greasy hair over her shoulder and leaned forward, conspiratorial.

"I'd chase 'im too if I were ten years younger." She cackled but stopped when the broker came out of his shop again. He dragged another box off the back of the cart and returned to the shop. "Me old man," she said with a jerk of her head. "Did this to me."

I gasped. "He killed you?" So much for keeping quiet.

"No. Well, not exactly, but 'e might as well 'ave. Got me

with child, 'e did, but I lost it. Lost it real bad, did all this." She spread out her nightdress. The blood formed a gruesome pattern. I glanced away, moved off. I didn't have time to chat to ghosts. Jacob needed me. "Then I died too," she went on. "But I can't leave. Not yet, not while 'e's prigging me sister. Scum, 'e is, but she don't know it."

Right. Very well. Not my business. "The other ghost," I whispered. "Did you see where he went?"

She pointed to a street opposite. "Chased that drunk down Bright Lane."

I nodded thanks and crossed the road to Bright Lane. I hesitated at the corner. Bright Lane was a misnomer. The street was barely a cart-width wide. It looked like it had been gouged out of the tenements that occupied either side of it. I doubted sunlight had touched the cobbles in the last century.

"Jacob?" I called softly.

He appeared at my side. "Give me the knife," he said. "When I call you, come in."

"Don't hurt George." But he'd already disappeared.

I was debating how long I should wait for his call when someone shouted. It sounded like George, swearing.

Then Jacob called. "Now!"

I ran into the gloom. It took a moment for my eyes to adjust to the darkness, but when they did, I almost smiled in relief. Jacob had George backed up against the brick wall, the knife to his throat. George—Mortlock—looked more annoyed than afraid, however, and a little drunk. He swayed and his eyelids sagged heavily.

"You," he said in disgust when he saw me. "Bloody freak." He pushed at the knife, but it cut his palm and he grunted. He flailed his arms wildly, trying to bat away Jacob's hand, but his fist went straight through the ghostly body.

"Come closer," Jacob urged me.

I did. Mortlock's gaze followed me. He licked his lips. "I'm going to have you." His grin was twisted until Jacob wiped it off by shoving the knife harder against his throat.

Mortlock cried out and tried to get away from the knife,

but that only made the blade sink in further. Blood dripped into his cravat.

"Jacob, don't hurt him!"

"Then do it now, Em," he snarled, "because I'm so very tempted."

"*Return to the Otherworld where you belong,*" I began, trying to keep my voice steady.

Mortlock's eyes widened. Jacob gave a short, gruff laugh of satisfaction.

I breathed in but paused as a putrid smell assaulted my nose. *Concentrate, Emily!* I began again. "*Return to—*"

A click of metal on metal came from behind me, loud in the tight, close space of Bright Lane.

Jacob looked past me. His gaze filled with dread.

I spun round. Someone dressed in a long, hooded cloak stood there, holding a gun. It was pointed at my chest.

"Put the knife down," the cloaked figure said in a whisper. "Or I'll shoot her."

CHAPTER 11

It was impossible to tell if the figure was male or female, thin or fat. The long cloak hid everything but the booted feet. The hood covered the eyes and the cloak's collar was pulled over the chin and mouth, muffling the whispered words. The horrible smell seemed to be coming from him, or her.

"Back away," he or she said. "Or I will shoot her."

I wanted to turn around and see if Jacob complied, but I didn't dare move. Not with the gun pointing at my pounding chest.

"Maybe I'll shoot anyway. Teach you a lesson about life."

Jacob gave a small strangled sound. He must have lowered the knife because the whisperer nodded in approval and I could hear Mortlock let out a breath. He shuffled past, giving me a wide berth.

I felt Jacob move up behind me. His body seethed with barely contained anger. "Who are you?" he growled.

Of course the whisperer didn't respond. He or she couldn't see Jacob, only the knife. "Why are you doing this?" I asked.

The whisperer said nothing.

Mortlock squinted at the hooded figure. He'd lost George's glasses. "I'd buy you an ale, but I ain't got a penny."

He chuckled and headed toward the main street. "I'll be off. Got me some business to 'tend to."

The figure turned the gun on him. "Stop, or I'll shoot."

"No!" I shouted. "George!"

Jacob's arm snaked around my waist and he pressed himself into my back, reassuring. "Shhh, Em," he murmured into my hair. "Don't draw attention to yourself."

"But he'll kill George!"

Jacob's grip tightened. "And if you try to stop him, he'll kill you. Just wait."

"You can stop him. Knock the gun away."

"Too risky. It might go off. And I want to hear what he wants from Mortlock."

"Turn around," the villain said.

Mortlock turned. His glare was vicious, his lip curled into a snarl. There was nothing of George in those cold eyes, only Mortlock. "What do you want now?" he snapped at the hooded figure.

"I've been looking for you everywhere." The gloved fingers flexed around the gun handle. "You didn't do as I asked."

"I did."

"Not for long enough."

Mortlock *humphed*. "You want me to do it again?"

"Yes. I'll give you whatever you want."

Jacob swore softly. I folded my hand over his at my waist and linked our fingers.

"Whatever I want?" Mortlock stood near the entrance to the alley, very still. Not a single hair moved. Beyond him, people went about their business, oblivious to the horrible scene playing out in the shadows. "What if I want to kill someone?"

The hooded figure shrugged, nodded. "I won't stand in your way. Just do what I say and I'll let your host body live." Another shrug. "If you don't, then I kill it and you have to return."

Mortlock's spirit wasn't like Jacob's. He couldn't go

wherever he wanted unless he occupied a live body. In his ghost form, he could choose to haunt the immediate area where he died or go back to the Waiting Area. Mortlock knew it. Unless he agreed to the whisperer's plans, George would be shot and Mortlock would simply be returned. Neither I nor the whisperer was close enough for Mortlock to transfer to us.

"You do this thing for me properly," the whisperer said, "and then you can do what you want."

Slowly, slowly, a slippery smile spread across Mortlock's face. "Looks like you and me got a deal."

"Come with me." The whisperer's partially covered face turned to us, a shadow within a shadow. "But first...I have to remove the witness." He turned the gun on me.

I screamed. Jacob shoved me aside as a bullet whistled past my ear.

"Emily!" he cried, crouching over me. "Oh God, Emily!"

"I'm fine. Go! Stop him!" But the villain was already gone, Mortlock too.

Jacob let go of me and pressed the small knife into my palm. "Go out there where you can be seen. Don't talk to anyone. I'll be back." He blinked off.

I wandered back to the main street, looked left and right. A woman sat in a doorway, a rag that might have once been a shawl draped around her shoulders. She wore no hat and no gloves and the toes poked out of her boots. I was about to ask her which way the two men had gone, but she removed a gin bottle from under her skirts, put it to her lips and drank until it was empty. When the contents were drained, she closed her eyes and her head lolled forward. She snored loudly.

Across the road, outside the broker's shop, the ghost who'd lost her child waved at me. I joined her and quietly asked if she'd seen anyone come out of Bright Lane before me.

"Only that 'andsome ghost. Fine one, 'e is. For a toff."

"No one else before him?"

She shrugged. "Been inside wiv me old man." She chuckled. "Rattled a few pans, moved stuff 'round. Makes 'im mad, it does. And scared."

I edged away. She followed me and chatted about the life she'd had before she died. I stopped listening after she told me her parents had died when she was twelve and she'd turned to thieving and whoring to support herself and her younger sister. It wasn't that I didn't care; I could do nothing about it. The poor woman was dead. In many ways, she was better off than when she was alive.

Minutes ticked by and Jacob hadn't returned. The shopkeepers gave me odd looks as I walked back and forth in front of their windows. Most of the shops were empty. There was little money to spare in Shoreditch, even to purchase basic necessities. The shopkeepers were as poor and miserable as their customers, but at least their trade was honest. Perhaps.

"So she don't know no better, see. I gotta take care of 'er. She's me baby sister."

I blinked at the ghost. She had the sort of face that naturally sagged—long cheeks and bloodhound eyes—but it seemed to be dragged further down by the telling of her tale. She wiped her eyes even though she wasn't crying—ghosts couldn't—and promptly sank to the ground with a hopeless, dry sob.

I glanced back to her husband's shop. He stood in the doorway, smoking a pipe and watching me with undisguised interest. There was a meanness to his flat lips and yellow eyes, but otherwise he would have been handsome. He smiled, revealing two sharp teeth clamped around the pipe stem.

"You lost?" he called out without removing the pipe.

I signaled for the ghost to join me and I strode up to him. "No. I have business to conduct here. I'm a spirit medium."

"A what?"

"I see ghosts."

He grinned again. His pointed teeth were positively horrifying. "And I can pull tulips out of me arse."

My fingers felt for the tiny button to release the knife blade. I pressed it and held the blade up for him to see.

He laughed around the pipe. "That don't scare me, girlie."

"I tried cuttin' 'im once," the ghost said. "He just got a bigger knife and cut me instead."

He spread his arms out wide. "Come on, girlie, have a go."

I handed my weapon to the ghost.

The shopkeeper's mouth flopped open and his pipe fell out. It broke into two pieces on the pavement. "Wh..wha...what...?" He backed into the shop which suited me. That way no one else could see the floating knife. The ghost and I followed him inside. The small shop smelled damp with an underlying reek of tobacco. Old pans and kitchen utensils, most of them broken, lay scattered across a central table. Rags, clothes, and old boots spilled out of trunks and pieces of scrap iron hung from the ceiling like long leaves from a tree.

"What's your name?" I asked the ghost.

"Moll."

I smiled at the shopkeeper. He stared wide-eyed back at me. "Moll tells me you treated her badly when she was alive."

"Moll?" he echoed. "B...but...it *was* her movin' my stuff? I thought it was the wind..." He ended the sentence with a loud gulp.

I nodded at Moll and she held up the knife. He stepped back and tripped over a large copper pot. He landed in it, his legs dangling over the side.

"She's here and she's very angry that you're taking advantage of her sister."

"I'm not! I swear, I'm not!" He struggled to get out of the pot.

Moll thrust the knife under his nose. His face drained of color and he went cross-eyed trying to see the blade.

She laughed. "This is fun."

I glanced at the door. I needed to get outside and wait for Jacob. He wouldn't leave me alone for long in Shoreditch. "Don't go anywhere near Moll's sister again. If you don't do as I say, Moll will return and she won't hesitate to use that knife on you. Or do something much worse."

I let the unspecified threat hang in the air, allowing his imagination to fill in the particulars. It seemed to work. He nodded quickly.

"Don't go back on your word," I told the shaking shopkeeper. "She'll know."

He nodded again. Moll stepped away, then, just as her husband hauled himself out of the pot, she lunged. He covered his face, lost his balance and fell back into the pot.

Moll bent over double, laughing. "I could do this all day."

I signaled her to follow me outside and she did, still chuckling. "Is that enough for you to return to crossover?" I asked her.

She shrugged one shoulder. "S'pose. Been wanting to leave for a time now, but just couldn't. Not wiv 'im doin' me sister." She peered back into the shop. The shopkeeper had retreated behind the counter at the back, but he kept his yellow gaze on me. "Good riddance." She handed the knife back to me and disappeared.

I expelled a breath. How long would it be before the shopkeeper decided Moll was either gone or a figment of his imagination?

How long before he came after me?

I didn't fold the blade away but kept it ready and moved down the line of shops. When I reached the end, Jacob appeared.

"Are you all right?" he asked, looking me over. "Anything happen?"

"No."

"Then let's go."

"Did you find them?" I asked as we crossed the road.

He shook his head. "They just disappeared. I looked everywhere. Streets, houses, shops. Nowhere. They just vanished." He kicked the gutter. It would have broken the toes of a mortal person but not him. "I can't believe they got away."

They couldn't have vanished. It wasn't possible. So where had they gone? Perhaps if Jacob had more time to look, he might have found them. He'd probably thought he needed to return for me, to keep me safe.

"I'm sorry, Em," he said. It sounded so sad, so...final. Like he was apologizing for more than losing Mortlock and the cloaked figure.

I linked my hand through his and squeezed. "We'll find them."

We had to, and before they did something awful to Jacob's family. I suspected that Mortlock had been separated from the person who'd summoned him ever since his initial possession, and this was the first time they'd actually met. Anything could happen.

"So what do we do now?" I asked.

"Now I take you home."

There was nothing else for it but to comply. I couldn't think what to do to be useful. Jacob needed to search for Mortlock and he wouldn't do that until I was home safe.

Our hands remained linked until we caught the omnibus heading back toward Chelsea. A rough, fast ride later, we were dropped off around the corner from Druids Way. We walked in comfortable silence and I was happy to have it that way. Lately our conversations ended in harsh words or awkwardness. Saying nothing was better than arguing.

Then I remembered something I hadn't told him. Something that wouldn't cause an argument. "Celia and I found my grandfather."

I told Jacob about François Moreau and his daughter, my Aunt Cara, and how I'd chased her but lost her. Losing people was turning into a regular occurrence for me.

"Moreau didn't tell you where to find her?" he asked.

"No. He's mad. It was impossible to get straight answers out of him."

We turned into Druids Way and his fingers touched mine, but only for a very brief moment until he pulled away and stopped. "It's her," I said.

I saw her at the same time. Cara. She sat on the steps leading up to our door. Her unbound hair whipped about her face, obscuring or revealing it on the wind's whim. She spotted us too.

"I'll make sure she doesn't leave," Jacob said.

I caught his shirt sleeve. "Don't frighten her. I think she's waiting for us, but if we scare her, she might leave."

We walked quickly. I could feel the tension in Jacob as if he was prepared to spring after her if she ran away. But she didn't. She waited, clasping the frayed edges of her coat together at her chest with both hands. It was too small for her, the sleeves ending halfway between elbow and wrist, the hem not quite reaching her knee.

I greeted her with a tentative smile. "My name's Emily Chambers." I held out my hand.

She stood very still. Her hair was the only thing about her person that moved. Then she took my hand. Her gloveless fingers were freezing.

"I'm Cara Moreau," she said in a small voice.

Jacob introduced himself, but they didn't shake hands. She nodded and blinked up at him, her brown eyes huge in her oval face. Her fingers curled into her coat once more, pulling it tight.

"Come inside," I said. "The fire will be warm."

I could see her warring with herself. She wanted the warmth and wanted to talk to us, but she didn't trust us enough to enter into the lion's den, so to speak.

"Our maid makes excellent seed cake," I said. "And chocolate."

Her eyes lit up at the mention of chocolate. She nodded and followed me inside. Jacob came in last of all. I called for Lucy and she emerged from the kitchen at the back of the house, wiping her hands on her apron. She smiled a greeting and her gaze flicked to me then back to Cara then back to me again. She must have suspected we were related but said nothing. Not even her smile faltered.

"Lucy, is there any of your seed cake left?"

"Sorry, miss, it's all gone. But I just finished baking gingerbread. Shall I bring some in to the drawing room?"

"Yes, please, and chocolate for Miss Moreau and tea for me. Is Celia home?"

She nodded at the drawing room door. "In there, miss." She bustled off.

I took Cara in and introduced her to Celia. My sister shook her hand enthusiastically. "I'm so glad you came to us," she said. "We've been wanting to meet you ever since we learned of your existence."

Cara twisted her hands in her coat and shuffled her feet. Her gaze wandered around the room and settled on the fireplace. Jacob dragged one of the chairs closer and Cara sat. She spread her fingers toward the warmth as Jacob piled on more coal.

"We *are* glad you came to us," I said, sitting on the sofa. "We've been worried about you."

She frowned. "Why would you worry about me? I'm nobody."

Jacob and I exchanged glances. "You're not nobody to me," I said. "You're my aunt. The only one I have as far as I know."

That elicited a smile from her. "Papa told me about you after you chased me. He said you're my brother's daughter. I didn't even know I had a brother 'til then." Her smile widened. "So I'm your aunty."

"It is rather absurd, isn't it?" I said, laughing.

She giggled and suddenly seemed every bit the ten year-old girl. In the events of the past few days, it was easy to forget she was still a child.

"Your father never told you about Louis?" Celia asked. She sat beside me on the sofa, her hands clasped primly in her lap. If she weren't leaning forward slightly I would have thought she was simply making polite conversation and not particularly interested in the answer.

"No," Cara said. She looked down at the fire, now throwing its warmth generously into the room. "He doesn't say much about anything. Not what makes sense anyway."

Celia leaned back and sighed. Lucy came in with a tray laden with cups, teapot, chocolate pot, and gingerbread. She set the tea things out on the table beside Celia. The plate of gingerbreads, chocolate pot, and one cup she placed within Cara's reach. She stood back and watched but Cara didn't move.

"Go on, miss," Lucy urged. "It tastes good. Look, I'll pour." She poured steaming liquid chocolate into the cup.

Cara glanced at me. I nodded. Her small fingers closed around the cup and she held it for a moment, soaking up the warmth. She sipped. Her tongue dashed across her upper lip, lapping up any chocolate that clung to it. Then she drained the cup.

Lucy filled it again and left, taking the tray with her.

Celia poured tea for herself and me while Cara nibbled the corner of a piece of gingerbread. I watched, fascinated, as pleasure spread across her face and lit up her eyes. Seeing how such a simple thing brought her so much joy, I felt ashamed. Celia and I may not have much money, but we weren't destitute. If wandering through London's slums hadn't reminded me how lucky I was, then seeing Cara devour the gingerbread with such relish did.

Celia seemed to agree. She watched Cara over the rim of her cup, a curiously wistful expression on her face.

Jacob, on the other hand, paced around the room. Cara's gaze followed him.

"Jacob, please sit," I said. "You're making us nervous."

He stopped. "My apologies. I'm frustrated, that's all. I should be looking for Mortlock, but I don't know where to start."

"The spirit?" Cara asked, lowering her cup.

He nodded.

She bit her lip. "I brung him here. It's all my fault."

Beside me, Celia made a small sound, but I wasn't sure if it was due to the mention of Mortlock and Cara's involvement, or because of Cara's mangling of the English language.

Jacob crouched at Cara's knee so that she looked down at him and not up. "No," he said. "No, it's not your fault. That man ordered you to do it, didn't he?"

Tears welled in her eyes. Jacob lowered his head and shook it.

"Did he threaten you?" I asked Cara softly.

She sniffed. "He told me he'd hurt Papa if I didn't do what he said." She looked at me, her eyes like lakes. It was a miracle the tears didn't spill. "I got no one else, see. Just Papa. Before my Mam died, she took me to him. Told me he was my Papa and that when her time came I was to go to him. She only lived another week."

"You didn't know François Moreau before that?" Celia asked.

Cara shook her head. "He lets me sleep in the room next to his, but it's got no bed, just a mattress on the floor and it's itchy." She looked around her, at the fireplace, the furniture, up at the ceiling. "It's not like this."

Her story chilled me. My own relation living in such poverty and with a man she hardly knew. I felt ashamed of myself and my good fortune to have Celia. What might have become of me if my mother had told me to go live with François Moreau, my grandfather, after she died?

"He's not bad," Cara added. "He's crazy, but he makes enough money for us to eat. He lets me do what I want and never hits me. If that man hurt him...I don't know where I'd live."

"What did he look like?" Jacob asked. He was still crouched before her.

She shrugged. "Don't know. I never saw a face. He kept the hood low over his eyes and the collar up. And he whispered." She whispered too. "Never said nothing out loud. 'Spose he was trying to hide his voice."

"Is there anything else about him that you found distinctive?" I asked. "Has he said anything that might give us a clue as to who he is or where he lives?"

She shrugged again. "He's a toff. Speaks nice, like you. Not from the East End."

"What about Mortlock?" Jacob asked. "Do you know of any connection between them?"

She shook her head. "He wanted only Mortlock. Made me summon him and put him into that lady's body." She nodded at the window which looked out to Druids Way and the spot where Mortlock first possessed Adelaide. "Told me the spirit had to go in her, no one else. I don't know why."

Jacob slowly stood. Cara watched him, her cup still clasped between her hands. She pressed the rim to her lips but didn't sip.

"Who is she?" she whispered. "That lady in the pretty dress?"

"My sister," Jacob said. "The other woman was my mother."

Cara nodded and blinked up at him. "Is she...is she all right?"

He nodded and gave her a reassuring smile. "She doesn't remember much of it."

"Good. I didn't know what would happen. I've never done that before. Never got a spirit inside someone." She glanced at me and I shook my head. I hadn't done it either. "There's no one else like us, is there? No one who can see what we see." She nodded at Jacob.

"As far as I know, we're the only ones. It's an old family trick apparently. It makes us special." It was something Mama used to say whenever I lamented my talent. Celia had taken up the mantra after our mother's death. I didn't believe it then and I still didn't.

"I don't like being special," Cara said, peering into her cup. "Not when people make me call the horrible spirits like Mr. Mortlock." She shivered and her knuckles whitened around the cup. "I don't like him. I wish he stayed dead."

I got up and crouched in front of her the way Jacob had. "He's still dead," I said. "All we have to do is send him back. Jacob will find him."

She glanced at Jacob. "You said you don't know where he is."

"We lost him in Shoreditch," he said.

I thanked God that Celia couldn't hear him. If she knew I'd been in Shoreditch with only a ghost to protect me, she'd have quite a few words to say about it and I wasn't in the mood for a lecture.

I rose and stood beside Jacob. He moved closer at first, then, as if he realized what he'd unconsciously done, he stepped back. Now that I was home, safe, he seemed eager to distance himself from me again.

"Did Mr. Beaufort just say something?" Celia asked.

I apologized to her. It must be frustrating to be the only one in the room who couldn't hear the entire conversation. I told her what had happened, excluding the parts about the gun, the location, and the threats. The recount ended up being very brief. "They just disappeared."

"They can't just disappear," she said.

"Yes, they can," Cara said. "And I know how."

CHAPTER 12

"How?" Celia, Jacob, and I asked as one.

Cara's shoulders squared and her eyes brightened. She seemed to be enjoying the attention, growing more confident. "Was there a hole in the ground?" she asked.

Jacob took a step toward her. "What kind of hole?"

"A hole in the street. Was there one near where you saw Mr. Mortlock?"

Jacob and I exchanged glances. He shrugged. "We don't know what sort of a hole you mean."

She rolled her eyes as if we were the most stupid people in England. "There are holes that go into the ground. I know some boys what went in one once and said it stinks down there. They said there's tunnels under the whole of London where monsters live. I told them there's no such thing as monsters," she said with all the superiority of an adult admonishing a foolish child. "I'd be able to see 'em, wouldn't I, since I can see ghosts, and I've never met a monster."

"Do you mean manholes?" Celia asked.

"The sewers!" Jacob said.

The London sewer system was not a subject in which I was well versed. All I did know was that the sewers existed beneath the city and took London's refuse away. Our air would smell a great deal worse without them. I also knew there were manholes covered with heavy lids that could be used by the flushers—the sewer workers—to access the network of tunnels.

"That's why he smelled," I said. "The hooded person when he found us. Remember, Jacob? He stank."

"I can't smell," he said.

"Lucky you. He reeked."

"There must be a manhole near that lane," he said. "I'll take a look."

"They're probably long gone," I said. "They could be anywhere by now."

"I have to start somewhere." He disappeared.

"He's gone," I said for Celia's sake.

"I hope he finds them," she said. "Before something awful happens to Lady Preston or Adelaide."

Cara carefully put her cup down on the table and stood. "I'm sorry," she mumbled. Her earlier confidence had vanished and she seemed to fold in on herself as if she were trying to keep warm. "So awful sorry." She looked down at her feet and pulled the edges of her coat together.

"It's all right." I put my arm around her shoulders. "You mustn't blame yourself. That man took advantage of you. *He's* the one who should be sorry."

She nodded, but I could see she wasn't convinced. "I've got to go now."

"Wait," Celia said. Cara looked up. "Why did you come here, now, to Emily? You ran away yesterday, but today you sought her out. Why?"

Cara glanced over her shoulder as if she would run off again, but then she sniffed and tilted her chin at my sister. "When Papa told me I had more family, not just him, I wanted to come see for myself. See what you were like." She shrugged. "I knew you could see ghosts too, but I didn't know you was family until Papa said. Papa's good to me, he takes care of me." She shrugged again. "But he's crazy. He talks a lot of gibberish. He laughs like he told a joke, but it's not funny." Her eyes lifted to mine. "I wanted to see if you were nice. If you could tell me why I can see ghosts and how I can get that person to stay away from me, that one with the hood over his eyes. I don't like getting bad ghosts for him."

Poor girl. I'd always considered myself to be alone, a sort of lost soul who didn't belong in Celia's polite, genteel world but didn't belong elsewhere either. I was wrong. I was lucky to have Celia, to have a safe home. Cara was far worse off than I.

She peeled away from me. At the door she gave us an awkward curtsy. "Thank you for the chocolate and gingerbread. They were very nice." She turned to go.

"Wait!" Celia and I said together. "Stay," Celia added.

I was surprised that my usually cautious sister had the same thought as me. It would seem she believed Cara's story and believed the girl would not run away with our few valuables in the middle of the night.

Cara looked past her to me. She sucked in her bottom lip. Her huge eyes didn't blink.

I nodded encouragement. "We want you to stay with us. As you said, we're family and I'd feel happier knowing you were here, safe and warm." And not living with that mad old man in semi-squalid conditions.

"Emily's right," Celia said. "So will you stay? You'll have your own room with a proper bed. I'm sure my sister will give up her dolls for you to play with if you like."

"I'm too old for dolls," Cara said. "Will you teach me stuff? Numbers and letters and other things?"

Celia clapped her hands in delight. "Of course! Oh, it'll be so much fun for all of us." My sister might not enjoy the more complicated matters learned from museums and thick books, but teaching a young charge the necessities required to keep house was precisely the sort of thing she enjoyed. If she had her way, little Cara would be turned into a suitable marriage prospect by the time she was my age. Celia might even succeed with her.

Before Cara could say anything more on the subject,

Celia rang for Lucy. "Your room is on the next level up, same as ours," she said as we waited. "Now. The first thing you'll need is a bath. A warm one. Lucy will help you." She tapped her finger on her lips then took Cara by the shoulders and gently spun her round. "You'll need clothes. There might be an old dress of Emily's that'll fit. I'll look in the attic while you bathe."

Lucy arrived and all three bustled out of the drawing room and up the stairs. I returned to the sofa and tried to occupy myself with embroidery. Unfortunately, while my hands were busy, my mind wandered. I kept worrying about Jacob finding Mortlock, wondering if we could stop him before the horrid spirit did something awful to the Beauforts. I did come to the conclusion that the hooded figure wouldn't direct Mortlock to kill Jacob's family. If he'd wanted to do that, he could have tried himself. More likely he would return to the original plan of ruining them by having Mortlock possess Adelaide again and force her to do something terrible. Some things were worse than death.

That didn't mean Mortlock wouldn't take it upon himself to murder them anyway. The spirit was extremely unpredictable and sinister.

I was saved from my dark thoughts by a knock at the door. It was Theo, smiling. I smiled back, glad to see him.

"I'm so relieved to see you're all right," he said.

"How kind of you to say so."

He removed his hat and cleared his throat. "Ever since you left my aunt's house, I've been concerned. I know it's growing late in the day, but I had to check on you."

"Thank you. As you can see, I'm well."

His gaze raked over me. Lingering. Burning. I felt hot, inside and out.

"So I see," he said, thickly.

I swallowed. "Please come in and have tea."

I ushered him into the drawing room. He paused at the door and took in the surroundings. I was suddenly conscious of the faded sofa, the thinning carpet and smallness of the room. It was a new sensation for me. Unlike Celia, I'd never felt ashamed of our modest house before. Perhaps my embarrassment now was because Jacob had said Theo needed to marry a rich heiress and I felt Theo was judging me on what I had to offer.

But that was silly—I didn't want to wed Theo. So why was I suddenly so awkward?

"Is this a bad time?" he asked, settling on the chair Cara had vacated near the fire.

"Not at all. Lucy and Celia are occupied with Cara. She's going to live with us."

"Cara?"

I poured tea and recounted recent events up to and including Jacob's current adventure in the sewers.

"So I am just waiting here," I said with a sigh.

He grinned. "How frustrating for a person of activity such as yourself."

A person of activity. I liked it. "So what do you think of me being the niece of a ten year-old girl?"

"I think she is very lucky to have you and your sister as family."

I offered him the plate of gingerbread and he took a piece. "She might not think so after Celia's attempts to turn her into a fine young lady."

He laughed again and bit into the gingerbread. Neither of us spoke as he chewed and the silence didn't sit naturally. I felt like I needed to fill it, so I asked him a question I wanted to take back.

"What do you think of our little house? Humble, is it not?" I groaned on the inside. Why did I have to draw attention to our meager residence?

Perhaps because his reaction to it had been on my mind ever since he'd arrived. And I wanted to know if there was any truth to what Jacob had said.

"Very comfortable." He gave me a smile. It made his eyes sparkle.

I smiled back, relieved. If he thought our house and

belongings shabby, he made no sign of it and no attempt to get away. Surely if Jacob was right and Theo didn't consider me a serious prospect now that he'd seen my house, he would have politely made excuses and left already.

But he hadn't. He was sipping tea, eating gingerbread, and making me feel beautiful and special by stealing glances my way.

The fact I was happy about it was unnerving. I *should* be making myself as undesirable to him as possible if I truly didn't want to contemplate marriage.

So why wasn't I?

"Your aunt told my sister you are going to study law," I said. "When do you start?"

"Next week." He picked up the teacup. It looked much too fragile for his big hands. "I'm looking forward to it." He sipped.

"And what area of law are you hoping to go into when you're finished?"

We chatted for a while longer. It was polite and rather bland, but just the sort of conversation a young gentleman and lady were expected to have together. Celia joined us and pretended not to listen, but her small smile of triumph told me all I needed to know. Not only was she listening, she was most likely planning our wedding.

Just as Theo got up to leave, Jacob appeared. Predictably, he scowled. "What's *he* doing here?"

I should have told Theo and Celia that Jacob was there, but I didn't. I was in no mood for a conversation between them all and I didn't particularly want Theo to linger now that Jacob had shown up. Anything could happen.

I said goodbye to Theo at the door then turned to Jacob standing behind me in the entrance hall. He spoke first. "I hope your sister has been with you the entire time as chaperone."

"Of course," I lied. "Not that it's any business of yours. You've made your feelings quite clear. Well, not clear exactly but..." I wanted him to tell me one way or another how he felt to lay my concerns to rest, but he did nothing of the sort.

"Emily," he said.

I waited. He obviously had something he needed to say and I wasn't going to make it easy for him. He paced across the hall, one side to the other in two big strides, and back again.

I gave up. I wasn't very good at feigning disinterest. "At least change course," I said. "You'll wear the carpet thin if you don't."

From the look he gave me, I didn't think my attempt at humor was appreciated. "You won't like what I have to say."

"That hasn't stopped you before."

"I've been asking around in the Waiting Area if anyone knew Theo."

"You did *what?*"

"Nobody did," he said.

I stalked off to the drawing room but remembered Celia was in there so I turned back to Jacob and kept my voice low. "I can't believe you would do that! *Why* would you do that?"

Hands on hips, feet slightly apart and defiance in his glare, he said, "Because I need to know what he's really like. I need to know if he's going to be good for you."

I choked on all the words jostling to spill out of my mouth. In the end I said nothing, just shook my head over and over at him.

Without changing his stance, he shrugged one shoulder. "Any spirit in my position would do the same."

"No, Jacob, they wouldn't. I'm just glad you didn't learn anything."

"Not there I didn't."

"Pardon?"

"I had to listen in to his conversation with his cousin to find out what I wanted to know."

My eyes widened so far my eyeballs hurt. "Oh, Jacob, that's not very nice."

The only movement he made was a slight flexing of the

muscles in his arms now crossed over his chest. "The normal rules of humanity don't apply to me anymore, Em."

"That's wrong, and you know it." I was so angry with him, my voice shook. It was difficult to keep it controlled, soft, so that Celia wouldn't hear and interrupt us. "Don't pretend that death changes the rules. It's one thing to use your, your...ghostliness to find Mortlock or fight demons, but it's quite another to sneak up on perfectly innocent people and listen in to their private conversations."

His lips flattened. "Don't you want to hear what I discovered?"

"No!"

"I learned that Theo seduced a girl last summer."

"I said I don't want to know." I should have walked away but he would have followed me so I stayed. And heard.

"Everybody assumed they would wed. Then a wealthy young lady came to the village to visit a distant relation. Theo soon forgot his dalliance with the first girl and moved onto the lady. It broke the girl's heart apparently."

My breaths were loud in my ears, my pulse raced. I shouldn't be listening. The conversation had been a private one.

"By the end of summer," he went on, "it appeared Theo would wed the wealthy heiress instead. It would have settled all his family's problems. His father is in debt and can no longer support his grown son. Theo needs to find work, or marry well. But when summer ended, so did his chance of marrying the heiress. She left and he never heard from her again."

I was riveted to his story. It's a terrible thing to admit after the way I'd admonished him for his actions, and I was ashamed of myself. But not so ashamed that I walked away.

"You said you overheard this conversation between Theo and Wallace," I said carefully. "Were they telling it as if it were a joke? As if they cared nothing for the poor girl Theo ruined?"

Jacob sat on the bottom step of the staircase and

indicated I should sit with him so I did. We kept some distance between us, but it wasn't enough. It was never enough. I was very aware of him, of every subtle movement, especially his lack of breathing. "It wasn't a joke to either of them," he said. "Wallace didn't seem to know the entire story so Theo relayed it. He sounded genuinely sorry for his actions toward the girl. He seemed to have liked her but admitted he couldn't afford to marry her."

"He hadn't liked her enough," I said. "Hadn't loved her."

"It would seem so."

I wasn't looking at him, but I could feel him watching me. I kept my gaze on the carpet. "How do you know he didn't love the heiress?"

He stretched out his long legs, crossing them at the ankles. "Although he didn't speak unkindly about her, there wasn't any sense of loss or sadness either. I think there was more hurt pride than genuine sorrow."

I stretched my arms around my drawn-up knees. "So what are you saying, Jacob? Why are you telling me this?"

"As a warning. He seduced a girl and abandoned her when a better prospect came along."

"You don't know that for certain."

"I heard it from his lips!"

"But you didn't hear what his heart said. He might have loved the heiress more."

"Then why is he pursuing you? A few months is not long enough to get over a broken heart. If what you say is true, then he's fickle. He falls in and out of love when the wind changes direction."

"*You* are calling *him* fickle?" It was so ridiculous it was laughable. But I wasn't laughing. I was falling apart on the inside. "Last week you told me you loved me. This week you said you were mistaken."

"Emily, don't. Everything is different when you're dead. Everything."

The argument wasn't one I could ever win, not having experienced death first hand. "You cannot blacken his name forever because of one mistake, Jacob. He might be terribly remorseful and have learned his lesson."

He stood and held up his hands. "I just wanted to warn you. You need to be aware—"

"No, Jacob!" I sprang to my feet. "I do *not* need to be aware of one single incident. What happened last summer in a distant village is nothing to do with me, here and now."

"Don't get mad, Emily, I simply thought you should know what he's like—"

"I *do* know what he's like! He's kind to me, polite and thoughtful. He came to ask if I was all right. He's worried about my safety."

"And that makes him special?" he growled in a voice so low it rumbled through the air and vibrated across my skin. "I am not the enemy, Emily. I don't want to see him take advantage of you. I don't want the same thing that happened to that girl to happen to you."

"I'm not her, Jacob. I'm not penniless."

"You will be when you cease your performances. And I can assure you, Theo isn't the sort who'll want his betrothed to work as a spirit medium. I doubt he'll want to work either."

"Oh, you can assure me, can you? That's comforting." I shivered and my eyes burned with tears. Didn't he understand what he was saying, how hurtful he was being? "He is going to be a lawyer."

"Perhaps."

My lip wobbled and I bit it. He frowned, half-shook his head. He didn't understand at all. It would seem I had to spell it out to him. "Is it so difficult to believe that he couldn't love me enough to give up his life of idleness? Do you think me that unlovable?"

His mouth opened and closed, opened and closed like an automaton. "That's not what I meant."

The tears spilled down my cheeks in a torrent. I couldn't stop them. No matter how quickly I dashed them away, new ones followed. It was childish and humiliating, but I was *so* angry. And sad. I turned to run up the stairs.

He caught my shoulders, not hard but not gently either. I tried to shake him off, but his grip tightened. "Emily, no." He whispered. Even with him pressed against my back I could barely hear him. "Don't. Please. That's not what I meant. Don't cry."

I tried again to shake his hands off and this time he let go. I ran up the stairs, passing Cara and Lucy on their way down.

"Miss Chambers?" Lucy said to my retreating back. "Everything all right?"

"What did you say to her?" It was Cara, her girlish voice filled with righteous anger. I imagined her little finger pointing at Jacob. "Well, mister?" she shouted.

"Th...the ghost is here?" That was Lucy. She whimpered. She'd probably gone as white as her apron, perhaps even plopped down on the step.

Just as I opened the door to my room, I heard Celia's voice. "Young ladies do not shout, Cara."

"But *he* made Miss Emily cry."

I didn't hear my sister's response. Or Jacob's. I slammed the door on them all. The things on my dressing table rattled and the framed embroidery on the wall slipped on its hook and resettled crookedly.

Then I threw myself on my bed and wept into my pillow. It was bad enough thinking about what he'd said. It was even worse knowing I had to face him again soon.

Mortlock had to be sent back before he did something terrible to Adelaide. He wasn't going to wait for my heart to heal.

CHAPTER 13

Cara ate a small mountain of toast for breakfast. It was just as well that she was hungry because I wasn't and Celia was too pre-occupied with replenishing Cara's plate to notice.

I, on the other hand, was too pre-occupied thinking about Jacob. Had I been unfair? After all, he never *said* I was unlovable. It's just that his reaction to Theo had been rather odd. Was he trying to protect me from a future pain if Theo's attentions came to nothing, or was he simply jealous? My hopes were pinned on jealous.

"He left straight away." Cara shoved the last piece of toast into her mouth. "Mr. Beaufort the ghost," she added, spraying soggy crumbs onto her plate.

"Cara dear," Celia said with far more patience than she would have shown me, "ladies do not speak with full mouths."

Cara swallowed hard and stretched out her neck as if she could force the toast down faster. "But I'm no lady."

"Not yet," my sister said. "But you will be." She spoke with a determination that dared us to counter her. I knew better than to try, and Cara simply blinked her long lashes over big brown eyes and nodded in earnest. She seemed to be drinking up my sister's enthusiasm, which no doubt accounted for the air of satisfaction in Celia's manner this morning.

"Did he say anything before he left?" I asked Cara. I couldn't help it. I had to know everything about Jacob, everything he said and did, and now I had an ally who could see and hear him when I wasn't there. Despite my aching heart, I felt a flood of affection for the girl. I was no longer alone, no longer the only freak in London. We had each other, and we both had Celia. I was feeling very fortunate on that score.

"He said he was sorry and he didn't like making you cry." Cara screwed up her nose. "I s'pose he looked sorry too. Kind of sad."

I swallowed the lump in my throat. "Did he say anything else?"

"He said he would come back today after he found that mean spirit, Mortlock," Celia said. "I hope it's soon."

"So do I," I murmured.

After breakfast, I urged Celia to take Cara out. If Jacob returned, I didn't want her around. She might insist on helping send Mortlock back since she felt partially responsible for his presence, and I did not want to endanger her life too. Celia agreed, albeit reluctantly. With a grim set to her mouth, she took my hand and squeezed it. The look she gave me told me everything I needed to know without words passing between us: *be careful*.

Cara didn't ask questions when Celia told her they would go shopping for some new clothes. She bounced on her toes, squealed in delight and hugged my sister tightly. Celia smiled down at her with a soft shine in her eyes then pried the girl's arms from around her waist.

"We cannot afford much," she warned Cara. "But I think our budget can stretch to a new set of underthings and some fabric for a new dress. As to a new coat, you will have to wear one of Emily's old ones for now."

"Yes, Miss Chambers," Cara said. Her smile was almost too wide for her face as she trotted behind Celia.

I didn't have to wait long for Jacob to appear. I was

shocked to see him. I didn't think a ghost could look haggard, but there was a bone-deep weariness to him that made my heart swell.

I went to him and he wordlessly enclosed me in his arms, resting his chin on the top of my head. I breathed deeply, drawing air into my lungs but not his scent. He had none. I felt his body relax into mine and it felt good to just hold him and be held by him. I hated arguing all the time.

"I'm sorry," he finally said in a rasping voice I barely recognized.

"It's not your fault. I...overreacted. I know you didn't mean I'm not unlovable."

The corded muscles in his arms tensed. "It is the one thing I could never say about you." He gently pushed me away but held onto my arms. His thumbs caressed my sleeves and his eyes searched mine, until once more something came over him. His features hardened and he let go of me. "I found Mortlock," he said. "We must leave. Now."

The unresolved feelings between us would have to remain that way. Mortlock had to be our first priority.

I threw on my coat and hurried after him. We walked side by side to St. James's Street and I listened as Jacob told me how he'd stayed all night at his parents' house, a weapon nearby, and waited for Mortlock. But the spirit possessing George's body had not arrived and when dawn peeped over the rooftops and the servants stirred, he left in search of him. He'd found him at a gentleman's club in St. James's Street. Mortlock must have realized George probably belonged to one of the exclusive clubs where he could find a bed and dine like a prince on George's credit. Jacob had visited each club in turn until he found him.

I watched from across the street as Jacob went inside to flush Mortlock out. The gloomy mist clung to my clothes and turned my hair into a frizzy mess in the five minutes it took for him to reappear beside me.

"He's not there," he said.

"You must go in search of him again." I was about to add that he couldn't have gone far, but that may not have been true. If Mortlock had caught an omnibus, he could be out of London already. "Your family..."

He nodded and scrubbed a hand through his dark hair. "I'll check on them now. Emily..." An intense sadness settled into his eyes and I thought he would kiss me, but he didn't. He tugged on the collar of my coat, his knuckle brushing the underside of my jaw, and said, "Go home. Stay warm." And then he was gone.

I trudged home, trying yet again to sift through my tumultuous emotions. I was so engrossed that I failed to notice Theo approaching from the opposite direction along Druids Way.

"Emily!" He greeted me with a bow. "I was just coming to see you."

"Is everything all right?"

"Fine, fine. I came to ask how you progress with Mortlock. Did Jacob find him?"

I was about to update him with the morning's news when a scream tore through the mist. It came from the direction of my house.

"Lucy!" I shouted.

We raced inside and found Lucy on the drawing room sofa, Mortlock in George's body on top of her. His hand covered her mouth and her skirts were up around her thighs. She thrashed beneath him but not vigorously. Her dazed expression and the bruises blooming on her face told us why—he'd beaten her until she'd almost passed out.

My gasp turned Mortlock's head. He gave us a twisted smile, a predatory gleam in his eyes. He shifted his weight, showing us the knife in his hand. He shoved it under Lucy's chin and she whimpered and jerked her head back.

"It's all right, Lucy," I soothed. "We won't let him hurt you."

"You want to risk that?" Mortlock squinted past me to Theo. I'd forgotten he'd lost George's glasses. How much could he see without them? "Who's your lover?"

Theo stepped in front of me. "Let her go," he said.

"Or what?"

"I'll send you back," I said. I concentrated on steadying my breathing, wishing I felt as calm as I sounded.

Lucy groaned again. Her bosom heaved beneath her apron and her cap had fallen off somewhere so that her pale hair fanned around her. She looked like the poor victim in a Gothic novel, sublime yet tragic. I would not let Mortlock hurt her.

I inched closer. How close did I need to be to send him back? How close did I dare get?

"No, Emily," Theo warned, once more stepping in front of me. "Stay back. Let me handle him." He undid his topmost coat buttons.

"No, I must send him back," I said. Oh God, where was Jacob? I desperately wanted to call for him. He could sneak up on Mortlock and use a weapon, but I knew that as soon as his name passed my lips, Mortlock would cut Lucy. The risk was too great.

As was the risk of Theo fighting him, or trying to. But he continued to undo his coat, his fierce glare stripped of all its usual good humor. There was a viciousness there that almost matched Mortlock's. Almost.

Mortlock simply laughed. "Come on, boy, let's see if you're man enough."

Theo growled and threw his coat to the side.

"No!" I caught his arm and used all my strength to hold him back. "He'll hurt her." To Mortlock, I said, "Let me swap with her. You don't want her, do you? You want me. You want to hurt *me*, Mr. Mortlock."

I had his interest although he didn't set aside the knife. He licked his lips and grinned like I'd never seen George grin before. It was full of malice and at that moment, I knew evil existed. "God yes." He chuckled low in his throat. "You're a pretty little thing for a darky. I'm going to hurt you bad, see if you bleed red like a pure white girl. Then I'll make you beg me on your knees."

"Enough!" snapped Theo.

Lucy screamed as the knife dug into the flesh at her throat. Blood seeped from the wound and trickled down to her heaving chest. "Please, miss, don't let him hurt me," she babbled through her sobs.

I approached him carefully, my hands out in front of me. "Swap," I said. "Her for me."

Theo tried to pull me back just as Mortlock grabbed my hands and jerked me forward onto the sofa. Lucy scrambled away and ran for the door, tears streaming down her cheeks. She was gone, safe. And I was touching Mortlock. It was close enough, I knew that for certain.

"Go back—"

My words were slapped from my mouth by the back of Mortlock's hand. I cried out and fell onto the sofa. My ears rang and fierce pain ripped across my jaw, still bruised from his beating mere days earlier. I closed my eyes to hold the stinging tears in check.

"You bastard!" Theo cried.

I opened my eyes to see him throw himself at Mortlock, shoving him to the side. The knife skimmed across my thigh then fell out of Mortlock's hand when he landed heavily on the floor. They struggled on the ground, each trying to get the upper hand. George wasn't a strongly built man, but Mortlock had lived on the cruel London streets for many years. He knew how to fight. He punched Theo, the blow snapping Theo's head back. It hit the floor with a thud and Theo's eyes fluttered closed. He'd lost consciousness.

It was up to me. "Go back—"

Mortlock leapt up and punched me across the face. "Stop," he growled. "Before I knock all those pretty white teeth out."

I couldn't stop. Couldn't afford to. There was no one else but me. I sucked in precious air to steady my rapid heartbeat and began again. But just as I opened my mouth to utter the words again, long, fine fingers wrapped around my throat.

George's fingers but Mortlock's intent. All the air whooshed out of me. I couldn't breathe, couldn't move. I needed air. My lungs begged for it, my chest tightened, burned. I scrabbled at his hands, clawing until I felt blood and skin beneath my fingernails but still he held me down by my throat. Crushing. I couldn't utter a single word to send him back or call Jacob.

I was utterly powerless.

Theo! Wake up, Theo!

"This'll work a charm it will," Mortlock said, laughing now as he pressed down. "I know it. Beaufort'll hate it, hate hisself, for not bein' 'ere to save you. It'll eat 'im up, just like I said it would." What did he mean? What was he saying? I couldn't focus on his words, their meaning. Everything was slipping away.

The room dimmed. I couldn't keep my eyes open. They were too heavy, as if a great weight forced them closed. Sleep. Blissful, heavenly slumber called me, and I could feel myself succumbing. I wanted to.

Then suddenly Mortlock let go. The room and the world returned with a loud rush like a steam train at full speed. Everyone seemed to be shouting or screaming. Lucy, Theo, Mortlock, and Jacob. Jacob!

Lucy helped me to sit up. I swayed against her and gingerly touched my throat. It hurt, but at least I could breathe again. Gasp after gasp of beautiful air filled my chest. As I watched, Theo grabbed Mortlock's arms from behind, pinning him to his chest. Jacob stood in front of him, the knife now in his hand, pressed up against Mortlock's cheek.

"You all right, miss?" Lucy asked, hugging me. "You were as white as me, you was, and you wasn't moving. I was so worried." She burst into tears and I wrapped my arms around her and she wrapped hers around me.

"Emily?" Jacob said at the same time Theo asked if I was all right. "Emily, say something."

"I'm well enough." The words scratched my throat and came out a harsh whisper.

A look of pain passed over Jacob's face, but it was fleeting, replaced by cold ruthlessness like I'd never seen. He said nothing, but I knew it would take a magician to get past him now. He would not allow Mortlock to escape this time.

"I ought to gut you for hurting her," Theo said, his voice low and ominous. He jerked backward, pulling Mortlock's arms hard and awkwardly. It must have hurt, but it was George he was hurting, not Mortlock.

"Say the words, Emily," Jacob said to me. "Send him back."

Gladly. But first, we needed answers. He was our only chance to learn the identity of Jacob's killer. "Who had the girl summon you?" I asked him.

Mortlock said nothing. He just laughed and closed his eyes. His face suddenly went blank.

"He's preparing to transfer to Hyde!" Jacob shouted.

There was no time to question him. If he transferred to Theo, then he would have a better chance of getting free. Jacob could only use weapons, not fists, and so without a second strong man to help, he was limited in what he could do. George would be dazed and useless for some time after Mortlock left him, if Wallace Arbuthnot's experience was an indication.

"Go back to whence you came," I chanted, moving closer as I did so. "Return, spirit." I repeated the order over and over until finally George's body went limp and I saw the hazy, transparent spirit of Mortlock rise. He hovered briefly and shot me a look filled with venom.

"She can't save you," Mortlock's ghost said to Jacob. "You'll become nothin', not even a spirit. Your enemy will get revenge." A strong breeze whooshed past us, flapping my skirts, and whisked Mortlock away as if he were a puff of smoke.

Jacob lowered the knife but kept alert, his gaze darting around the room.

"Is he gone?" Lucy whispered.

"He's gone," I said and hugged her closer. "He won't be

coming back." I couldn't be sure of that and Jacob said nothing. He was looking at me now, and at Theo who approached. George sat on the sofa, rubbing his eyes and nursing his cut hand.

"Are you all right, Emily?" Theo asked, taking my hand. It was warm and such a comfort. I squeezed and he squeezed back and sighed heavily, as if he could finally relax. "You were marvelous. Very brave."

"As were you," I said. "Thank you for your assistance."

He tucked a strand of my wayward hair behind my ear. "No need to thank me. I was glad I could help. It was lucky Beaufort came by when he did."

Jacob placed the knife very deliberately on the table near George who was looking about him as if he'd just woken from a puzzling dream. Jacob did not meet my gaze.

"Where am I?" George asked, squinting. "Where are my glasses? You know I cannot see well without them. Emily, that is you, isn't it?"

I went to him and reassured him that all was well. I didn't want to tell him what had happened yet, so I simply brushed off his questions and asked Lucy to fetch tea if she was up to it. She bustled away, checking the hallway beyond before stepping through the door.

"Your throat," Jacob said. He regarded me through blue eyes darkened to the color of a storm cloud. "Does it hurt?"

I touched my throat. The skin was tender and raw. "A little."

"I'm going to fetch a doctor," Theo said. He held his hand up when I protested and strode out of the room.

I took up his coat, left forgotten on the floor, and went after him. "You shouldn't go out without this."

He accepted it and our hands touched. His fingers closed around mine. I looked up into his eyes and saw something in them that made my heart flutter. Something fierce and filled with longing. Before I could speak, he bent his head and kissed me on the lips. It was feather-light, like he was afraid I would break if he unleashed the desire I saw in his eyes.

But I could not kiss him back. Not with Jacob standing behind me. I didn't need to see him to know he was there, I was as acutely aware of him as always. Jacob's presence was more powerful than a flooded, raging river. I couldn't ignore it.

Theo seemed to sense my hesitation and pulled back. "I apologize," he muttered. "The emotion of the moment overtook me." He made to leave, but I caught his arm.

"Theo," I said but could say nothing more. What could I tell him? That the man I loved was watching us? That kissing Theo felt like betraying Jacob? That despite everything, I'd enjoyed it and wanted him to kiss me again?

I didn't know what to think let alone say, so I just gave him a weak smile.

"I'll return with the doctor," he said and left.

I closed the door but did not turn around. "You shouldn't have watched us," I said. "That wasn't fair."

It was a long time before Jacob finally spoke. "Emily," was all he said. There was so much heartache in the one word that I was compelled to turn around.

He too turned suddenly and I could not see his face. His shoulders, however, were slumped and his head hung low. "I have to go," he said. "The Administrators are calling me."

I blinked and he was gone. I watched the space where he had been until I felt composed enough to return to George. As I told him what had transpired, I could not stop thinking of one thing in particular, one thing that had nothing to do with Mortlock or the man who had controlled him: Jacob had saved my life. He did not want me to die anymore.

What that meant, I was too befuddled and suddenly too tired to decipher.

CHAPTER 14

The doctor applied a salve to my throat and Lucy's bruises. He gave all of us odd looks but said nothing about our injuries. Fortunately he'd left by the time Celia and Cara arrived home with their purchases. My sister took one look at me and sent Cara up to her room. My little aunt obeyed, but I suspect that was more because Lucy promised to bring her a cup of hot chocolate and a pouch full of marbles she'd found in the attic.

When the door closed on them, Celia rounded on me. "Is he gone?"

For a moment I wasn't sure if she meant Jacob or Mortlock but since she wasn't currently upset with the former, she must mean the latter. "He's gone. We sent him back."

"*You* sent him back," Theo said, and I felt my face heat upon hearing the pride in his voice.

Celia heard it too and, like a hawk spotting its prey, she went in for the kill. "My sister is a remarkable young lady, isn't she, Mr. Hyde?"

"Quite remarkable."

"I wholeheartedly concur," George said, rising. He was rather the worse for wear after his ordeal. Mortlock had not treated his body well. The beginnings of a scraggly beard had sprouted on his chin and a web of red lines crisscrossed the whites of his eyes. "I must apologize most vehemently for my behavior, Miss Chambers," he said, trying to brush off a dark patch of dirt on his sleeve and failing. "Emily has told me some of the things I did..." He shuddered and pulled a face.

"It was not your fault, Mr. Culvert," Celia said. "None of us blame you."

"Alas, I blame myself," he said on a sigh.

"Don't," Theo and I said together.

"If only I could have fought the villain!" George shook his head and sat down again, weary. "I always thought my mind would be strong enough to withstand an attempt of possession."

"I doubt any of us could," I said. I didn't want poor George to feel bad. He'd been through enough and he looked so forlorn. "Shall I send Lucy to fetch your coach to take you home?"

He gave me a smile of thanks but shook his head. "Your maid is needed here. I'll walk home. The air will do me good."

"I think you are overstating the restorative properties of a London pea-souper, George." I held my hands out to him and he took them. "Are you sure about the coach?"

"I'm sure. Perhaps the air won't be good for me, but the exercise will. I need to clear my head and I've not far to go."

He bid us farewell and Celia walked him to the door, leaving Theo and I alone together which I rather suspected was her intent.

"Are you all right?" Theo asked, frowning.

"My nerves are somewhat frayed, but they'll recover now that Mortlock is gone."

"Mortlock may be, but the one who summoned him is not." We settled on the sofa, side by side, our knees touching. "Emily, I am very concerned. Mortlock indicated that you are now the target, not Beaufort's family. Why is that do you think?"

I shrugged and didn't meet his gaze. I wasn't ready to tell him that I loved Jacob and that I suspected he still had feelings for me too, even though he was denying it of late. Mortlock must have thought killing me would hurt Jacob more than possessing a member of his family would.

The situation between my spirit and me was too uncertain to discuss with Theo, not to mention socially unacceptable. Besides, something told me not to mention it to this gentleman. I dared hardly admit to myself that it was because I liked Theo too and didn't want to ruin any chance I may have with him.

I pushed the thought aside. Jacob was the only one for me, whether he were alive or dead.

"Promise me you'll be careful," he said, fixing me with an earnest stare.

"I promise."

"And you will come to me if you need anything. I mean it, Emily. I am at your disposal." He gripped my hands and his stare grew fiercer, as if he could will me to obey him.

"You are very kind. Thank you, Theo."

His eyes softened and a small, guarded smile tugged at his mouth. "It is not kindness that motivates me." He glanced at the door, perhaps looking to see if Celia were returning. She did not and I suspected she would give us several minutes to ourselves.

I suddenly felt uneasy. If Theo declared himself, what should I say?

"Emily, you must know..." He cleared his throat. "You must have realized how much I admire you."

I blushed all the way to my scalp. Oh my. He really was going to do it. Dear lord, don't let Jacob pop in yet.

"I think you are a remarkable young woman and a very pretty one."

"Thank you," I said.

"I have enjoyed your friendship and I hope...I hope that we can...get to know each other better."

"Of course, Theo. I would like that."

He looked relieved. "I will be basing myself at my aunt's house while I study so I won't be far away."

"Your studies will keep you busy, I'm sure."

"Not too busy to see you." He lifted my hand to his lips and kissed it. "I should go. Take care, dearest Emily."

We rose and I turned toward the door but stopped dead. Jacob stood at the end of the sofa, watching me. But there was none of his usual arrogant confidence in his stance or his manner. He looked lost and lonely.

Our gazes held for a brief moment and then he turned away. His fingers dug into the sofa's back. If Theo looked, he would have seen the dents they made.

"Are you leaving us, Mr. Hyde?" Celia asked, breezing into the drawing room with a too-bright smile. "What a shame."

"I must return to my aunt's house." Theo bowed to each of us. "Good day, ladies."

"Celia, would you mind walking Theo to the door?"

Her smile slipped a little, but lifted again when she turned it on Theo. "Certainly. Mr. Hyde?"

Theo bowed to me again and left with Celia.

"You shouldn't listen in on the conversations of others," I said to Jacob. The fact I hadn't been aware of his presence unsettled me. Ordinarily I knew when he was in the room, even when I wasn't looking at him.

"You're right," he said quietly. "I am sorry. I didn't mean to, but...I couldn't help myself."

The tremble in his voice crushed any words of reproach I'd been about to say. I moved up behind him and placed my hands flat against his back. Muscle rippled with tension beneath his shirt. He heaved a sigh then slowly turned.

His eyes were shadowed once more beneath his long, thick lashes. Whatever emotions had troubled him were now tucked away, out of sight. "I was wrong," he said.

"About what?"

"About Theo."

"Oh." I didn't want to hear this, didn't want this conversation, not with Jacob. It was awkward and utterly wrong. I turned away, but he spun round and caught my shoulders. Gently but determinedly, he made me face him. I would not look into his eyes, however. I was only holding onto my dignity with a thread as it was.

"I want you to...to let him court you."

"Jacob, please," I whispered. "Don't."

"No, listen to me." He tilted my chin, forcing me to look up at him. A glossy sheen made his eyes shine and if I didn't know better, I'd have thought he was gripped by a fever. "He seems like a good man. Solid. Not idle as I first thought."

"Really?"

My sneer prodded a wince from him and I instantly regretted my tone. "I think he would make a fine lawyer." He swallowed. "And a fine husband."

"Jacob, stop it!" He allowed me to wriggle free, dropping his hands to his sides. I stepped back where I hoped his intensity couldn't suck me in again. "Why are you doing this now when before you were so against him?"

He sat on the sofa. He looked deflated, defeated. "There are many reasons. But mostly it's because he is a good man and I've seen the way he looks at you."

"How does he look at me?"

"The same way I do."

An iron claw gripped my heart. Its sharp talons pierced and squeezed. "You mentioned other reasons," I whispered. "Tell me, Jacob. Tell me why you're pushing me toward him, because I don't understand." I was angry now, my words harsh. But I thought he loved me and I wanted to know how he could want another man to wrap his arms around me, kiss me, lie with me. I know I couldn't stand by and watch another woman with Jacob if the roles were reversed.

"I want you to be happy, Emily. Is that so hard to understand?"

My lip trembled and I bit it. I shook my head. And yet, there was something else. I could hear it in his voice and see it in the way he didn't quite look at me. "Why do you think another man would make me happy when it's you I love?"

He flinched as if I'd struck him. "Love can be fleeting."

I dropped to my knees at his feet and caught his face in my hands. "If you think what we have is fleeting then I will go to Theo. Willingly." I searched his face, but he wrenched himself free.

"There is another reason," he said. "I must give you up, Emily. It will keep you safe."

Give you up. His words gnawed at me. They meant something, but I couldn't think what. "We don't know that," I said.

"We do." His voice was thick and ominous, like a thunderstorm rolling in. "I heard Mortlock. The person who killed me wants me to suffer. Thanks to Mortlock, he now knows how I feel about you and he knows hurting you will hurt me." He suddenly grabbed me and pulled me onto his lap. I barely had a chance to suck in a breath before he kissed me.

The kiss was possessive but not hard. All my pent-up longing and desire spilled into the kiss and I pressed myself into him, wanted to have more of him. I pushed his shirt off one shoulder and he groaned as I kissed his bare skin.

Then he set me aside and stood. He paced the room, dragging his hands through his hair, down his face. "This is why." He groaned.

Tears burned my eyes, clogged my throat. I said nothing, just sat on the sofa like a pathetic, forgotten doll.

"Emily, please." He stopped pacing and dropped to his knees in front of me, our positions exactly reversed from moments ago. "Please, you have to forget about me. Go to Theo." He took my hand and pressed it against his cheek. His eyelids fluttered closed and the lashes looked like small, perfect fans. "It's the best thing, the right thing. I have to give you up or neither of us can move on." His eyes sprang open and he fixed me with a heart-shattering stare. "And we have to move on, Em."

I was crying now, the tears falling freely. Despite all the sadness flowing out of me, I remembered what his words meant. "You think giving me up is what will break the curse."

The flame within him seemed to dim. He nodded. "My killer said I must give something up. Something dear to me. *You* are dear to me." He smiled gently and rested a hand on my knee. "The dearest."

I held my breath until my emotions subsided and I could think a little clearer. "Then if you are right, and our parting is the trigger for you to crossover, I will try and..." I could not say "forget you" because I could not forget. "I will give you up too."

He bent and kissed my knee where his hand had been. "I do want you to be happy too," he said.

If my heart hadn't felt so heavy I would have laughed at that. "I know, Jacob. I know."

"And you will...let Theo court you?"

"I will let events run their natural course." I couldn't make promises in my current state. I certainly didn't feel like having another man court me, but it seemed to be important to Jacob that I give Theo the opportunity.

"His actions here today have convinced me he cares for you. Make sure he proves his worth though," he said, sounding like an older brother and not at all like the man I loved.

I nodded and wished the subject could be forgotten. "Will I see you again?"

"Of course," he said, much too cheerfully and quickly for me to believe him. "I will not cross without coming to see you first and I don't think I'll be going anywhere until the villain is caught. I cannot leave knowing you and my family are vulnerable."

I leaned forward and kissed him lightly on the lips, just as Celia entered. She frowned at me but said nothing. Jacob rose and with a sad smile, blinked out of existence. I sat back with a heavy sigh.

Celia perched on the sofa beside me. "That Mr. Hyde told me how brave you were. He has a great deal of admiration for you."

I sighed again. I suddenly felt so tired. All I wanted to do was crawl into bed and sleep.

"He's very nice too," she said. "Very nice indeed."

"I know." I didn't want this conversation with her, not straight after having it with Jacob.

Jacob, my ghost. Would I see him again? I couldn't be sure and he hadn't sounded certain himself. I got the feeling he would only be back if my life were in danger.

"Will you accept Mr. Hyde's attentions if he comes courting?" Celia asked frankly.

Perhaps Jacob was right and being courted by another man at his urging would mean he could move on. It was worth trying, and flirting with Theo wouldn't be a hardship. I did like him. A lot. And while my feelings for him did not match those I had for Jacob, perhaps I could one day love him enough to be happy.

"Yes," I said. "I will."

LOOK OUT FOR

Evermore
The third EMILY CHAMBERS SPIRIT MEDIUM novel.

Other books by C.J. Archer:

The Medium (Emily Chambers Spirit Medium #1)

Possession (Emily Chambers Spirit Medium #2)

Evermore (Emily Chambers Spirit Medium #3)

Her Secret Desire (Lord Hawkesbury's Players #1)

Scandal's Mistress (Lord Hawkesbury's Players #2)

To Tempt The Devil (Lord Hawkesbury's Players #3)

Honor Bound (The Witchblade Chronicles #1)

Kiss Of Ash (The Witchblade Chronicles #2)

Redemption

Surrender

The Mercenary's Price

ABOUT THE AUTHOR

C.J. Archer has loved history and books for as long as she can remember and feels fortunate that she found a way to combine the two by making up stories. She has at various times worked as a librarian, IT support person and technical writer but in her heart has always been a fiction writer. C.J. spent her early childhood in the dramatic beauty of outback Queensland, Australia, but now lives in suburban Melbourne with her husband and two children.

She has written numerous historical romances for adults. Visit her website www.cjarcher.com for a complete list.

She loves to hear from readers. You can contact her in one of these ways:
Email: cjarcher.writes@gmail.com
Twitter: www.twitter.com/cj_archer
Facebook: www.facebook.com/cjarcher.writes

Archer, C. J.
Possession

DEC - - 2019

CPSIA information can be obtained
at www.ICGtesting.com
Printed in the USA
LVHW090703091219
639808LV00005B/125/P

9 780987 337238